DANA MARTON

SHEIK PROTECTOR

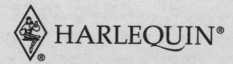

D0188542

HARLEQUIN®

TORONTO • NEW YORK • LONDON
AMSTERDAM • PARIS • SYDNEY • HAMBURG
STOCKHOLM • ATHENS • TOKYO • MILAN • MADRID
PRAGUE • WARSAW • BUDAPEST • AUCKLAND

If you purchased this book without a cover you should be aware that this book is stolen property. It was reported as "unsold and destroyed" to the publisher, and neither the author nor the publisher has received any payment for this "stripped book."

With many thanks to Denise Zaza, Allison Lyons, Maggie Scillia and Cindy Whitesel.

ISBN-13: 978-0-373-69352-8
ISBN-10:   0-373-69352-4

SHEIK PROTECTOR

Copyright © 2008 by Dana Marton

All rights reserved. Except for use in any review, the reproduction or utilization of this work in whole or in part in any form by any electronic, mechanical or other means, now known or hereafter invented, including xerography, photocopying and recording, or in any information storage or retrieval system, is forbidden without the written permission of the publisher, Harlequin Enterprises Limited, 225 Duncan Mill Road, Don Mills, Ontario, Canada M3B 3K9.

This is a work of fiction. Names, characters, places and incidents are either the product of the author's imagination or are used fictitiously, and any resemblance to actual persons, living or dead, business establishments, events or locales is entirely coincidental.

This edition published by arrangement with Harlequin Books S.A.

® and TM are trademarks of the publisher. Trademarks indicated with ® are registered in the United States Patent and Trademark Office, the Canadian Trade Marks Office and in other countries.

www.eHarlequin.com

Printed in U.S.A.

ABOUT THE AUTHOR

Dana Marton is the author of over a dozen fast-paced, action-adventure romantic suspense novels and a winner of the Daphne du Maurier Award of Excellence. She loves writing books of international intrigue, filled with dangerous plots that try her tough-as-nails heroes and the special women they fall in love with. Her books have been published in seven languages in eleven countries around the world. When not writing or reading, she loves to browse antique shops and enjoys working in her sizable flower garden where she searches for "bad" bugs with the skills of a superspy and vanquishes them with the agility of a commando soldier. Every day in her garden is a thriller. To find more information on her books, please visit www.danamarton.com. She would love to hear from her readers and can be reached via e-mail at DanaMarton@DanaMarton.com.

Books by Dana Marton

*Mission: Redemption

CAST OF CHARACTERS

Sheik Karim Abdullah—Fighting for his life is nothing new for the Dark Sheik; he's been escaping one assassination attempt after the other since early childhood. But the stakes have never been higher. This time, he has Julia Gardner and her unborn child to protect.

Julia Gardner—She came to Beharrain to find her child's father, but found his dominating brother instead. He is bent on protecting her, insisting on not letting her out of sight, let alone the country. Soon she is a target of assassins. Should she be running from Karim or toward him?

Mustafa—A holy man whose only purpose is to destroy what he considers evil and everyone who is connected to it.

Aziz Abdullah—Karim's twin brother was killed when an oil well was blown up by one of their own, their father's trusted man, who turned out to be their stepbrother.

Abdul Nidal—A shady merchant who deals in stolen antiquities. But is there more? Is he also involved in Aziz Abdullah's murder?

Tariq Abdullah—Karim's oldest brother and the only person he can unconditionally trust. Tariq was raised in the west and only recently returned to Beharrain, which brought some tension to the brothers' relationship and has since been resolved. He runs the tribe's oil business, MMPOIL.

Queen Dara—Beharrain's American-born queen is firmly on the side of peace and justice. Besides donating an amazing amount for children and women since marrying the king, she also started a government program for preserving the country's history.

Chapter One

"Car's rigged," Karim said to the empty passenger seat next to him. His gaze darted around as he considered his options for escape, trying to determine the location of the bomb.

He wished he could see under his seat. He wished he hadn't just tossed his briefcase, which held his cell phone, to the back, now out of reach. But most of all, he wished he hadn't gotten into the damned car.

Unfortunately, he had no magic lamp and no genie to grant his three wishes.

He sat completely still, sweat beading on his forehead. The first step was to figure out the trigger. Would the charge blow if he turned the key in the ignition, or if he got out and lifted his weight off the driver's seat? Maybe the trigger was in the door. He hadn't closed it behind him yet. Or could be he had no control at all. Maybe whoever wanted him dead was watching from one of the hundred windows that overlooked the executive parking lot. Watching with the remote in hand.

"I was getting too close to the truth." He glanced up at those windows, but couldn't see much from his position and he didn't dare shift his weight.

Anger flared. If he had to die, so be it—*Insha'Allah.* But by all that was holy, he wanted to bring his twin brother's murderer to justice first.

"I'm sorry, Aziz."

If he couldn't find the killer, nobody would. His other brother, Tariq, thought that Aziz's presence at the well at the time of the explosion had been a coincidence. Tariq was predisposed to see the world as a better place than it really was—he hadn't seen as much of the dark side as Karim—and was currently too busy being crazy in love with his new wife.

Which one of them was crazier remained to be seen. Karim's thoughts turned grim. He wasn't exactly a pillar of sanity, either. He regularly talked to his dead twin brother. For the last month, from time to time, he felt Aziz's presence so strongly, he not only talked to him, but also half expected an answer.

Aziz was gone. Killed. In some regard, losing his twin was like losing half his sight two decades ago, but much, much worse. With Aziz, he had lost half of his soul. And he knew he wasn't going to find that, even if he found the killer or killers—he wasn't going to bring Aziz back. Still, he could not let the bastards go free, not even if tracking them down cost him his own life.

A bomb.

"Should have seen it coming." Except that his mind

had been on the restitutions he was making to the families of the men who'd died at the well along with his brother.

If he hadn't been so preoccupied when he'd walked out of MMPOIL's headquarters in Tihrin—Beharrain's quickly growing capital—he would have noted that the security guard wasn't at his post. He hadn't been aware of danger until he'd gotten into the car and spotted the millimeter-size chunk of blue plastic wire coating on the mat.

Another person might not have realized the significance. But people had been trying to kill him from the moment he'd been born, nearly succeeding on a number of occasions. He'd developed a keen sense for detecting death's approaching footsteps.

He glanced out at the street, at the cars passing no more than a hundred feet from him. Nobody was turning to enter the company gate where the other security guard sat in his booth, his back to Karim.

He had to do something now, while he was alone in the parking lot. He didn't want to take anyone out with him.

"Here we go." His mind sharply focused, he reached down to feel around the seat, aware that he could accidentally move a wire and set off the charge if it was there.

He felt nothing out of place as far as he could reach, but he couldn't stretch all the way. *Next item.* He leaned forward carefully, and spent precious seconds inspecting the bottom of the dashboard.

"Mr. Abdullah?" The voice was richly melodic and completely feminine, utterly out of place in the charged tension of the moment. "Excuse me, Mr. Abdullah—"

He drew his attention from what he was doing to watch, with dismay, the foreign beauty who strode toward him, full of purpose.

Since she'd spoken English, he responded in the same language. "Go back inside."

"They told me I could find you here." She flashed a nervous smile and proceeded without pause, although the blood did drain from her face as she came closer and got a better look at him. "Look, I've come a long way. You wouldn't believe the plane ride. Forget the plane. You wouldn't believe the food," she babbled on. "I know you must be busy, but—"

"Get out of here." He didn't bother with the half turn to hide his scar, but looked her full in the face. That ought to scare her off.

"Listen, I—" Her voice wavered.

"You listen." He wiped the sweat from his forehead. The air was well over a hundred degrees outside, and even warmer in the car. He had run up to his office for only a few minutes to grab some papers before he headed off to the camel races, so he hadn't bothered to pull in to the climate-controlled underground parking garage. He let loose the frustration and anger that churned inside him. "Get the hell out of here. Now."

The woman stopped, but only momentarily. Her wide brown eyes flashed with determination, and her deep auburn hair swirled around her face in the dry breeze that'd been blowing from the desert all day. Hair that flowed in soft waves well below her elbows. Her soft linen skirt fluttered around her ankles, the light color matching her modest top—clothes that accentuated her tall, slim figure. She looked as beautiful as an angel and as determined as Satan's handmaiden.

Few men would have remained standing there when he had that glare on his face and that edge in his voice. But incomprehensibly, instead of running the other way, her delicate chin came up. She was maybe four feet from him and not budging.

"All I want—"

Oh, hell. "There's a bomb—" Karim saw movement in one of the windows behind her, and acted on instinct.

He vaulted out of the car and flew across the space between them, crashing her to the hard pavement, doing his best to break her fall. He didn't stop, but rolled and rolled.

She screamed the whole time and beat on his shoulders, resisted with all the power in her slim frame, her long hair entangling them. Then the car finally blew, shaking the parking lot.

Heat.

Smoke.

Fear.

She screamed even louder, but it barely registered now over the ringing in his ears.

Head down. He kept her covered as best he could, protected her from the burning debris that flew across the air like projectile missiles. As strong and determined as she had looked a moment ago, she seemed scared and fragile as she clung to him now.

"Don't move," he said near her ear, unable to hear his

own voice, half-deaf from the explosion. "It's okay." He made an attempt to reassure her anyway. They would assess their injuries and face reality in a moment. For now, he was still trying to catch his breath.

The air swirled blazing hot around them. But even the acrid smell of smoke couldn't completely drown out the scent of the woman in his arms: jasmine and vanilla.

In his peripheral vision, he registered security personnel running from the building.

"Ambulance. Now! Cover his position."

"Secure the grounds! Secure the grounds!"

"Are you all right, sir? Sheik?"

Karim let the woman go and nodded, the ringing in his ears diminishing with each passing second. She looked wide-eyed with shock, staring at the car a few short yards from them. Her fair skin was now positively white, to the point of being translucent, save a few smudges of dirt.

"What happened?" She pressed a hand to her abdomen, breathing in quick gasps.

He'd probably knocked the air out of her.

After checking her over for visible injuries and not finding any, he followed her gaze, clenching his teeth at the sight of the twisted metal behind him. That had been close. Too close. Aziz's death still filled his mind, dulling his attention to other things. He had to separate himself from the grief, had to block the memories of the burning well—a fire a thousand times larger than what burned in the parking lot now. He couldn't get distracted and be taken out. He had to find who killed Aziz.

The company's private ambulance was racing through the parking lot toward them. For him.

"I'm fine. You take her." Whatever she wanted from him, he had no time to deal with her now.

He'd spoken in Arabic, but she must have understood his body language, because she began to protest.

"No, I'm fine. Really. I don't need to see a doctor." She was rattled and scared, more than a little bewildered, fighting to hide it. Her chin came up, trembling slightly and smudged with dirt from the pavement. "I can't go." She backed away a few steps. "I'm not going."

The woman showed a deep-seated aversion to do as she was told. Even if it was for her own good.

He wasn't in the mood just now to humor her. "Get in."

Even his own security stilled at the growl in his voice.

"No," she said, oblivious to danger once again.

His eyes narrowed. Did she just stomp her feet or had she been flexing her knees?

He had been careful with her when he'd taken her down. She didn't look hurt. She was breathing normally now. Her clothes were barely rumpled and only slightly stained. Her hair looked the worst, tangled and with a fair amount of sand in it. The desert winds had been blowing for days, dusting the parking lot and everything else in the city.

His security force closed in a circle around them and awaited his orders. They would remove her forcefully; all he had to do was give the word. He should. He had a million things to do at the moment and no time for the distraction of a stubborn woman.

"Fine. No hospital," he said instead. "Just get in. Whoever did this could be still out here."

She paled even more, if that was possible, and stepped up into the back of the ambulance. He went after her, on second thought, not because he was scared for his life, but because if whoever was out there decided to shoot at him, the bastard might hit one of his men instead. Better to remove himself from sight.

"We can drop you off at your hotel. Please, sit." He gestured to the gurney. He remained standing, holding on to one of the restraints as the vehicle moved out. He nodded toward the lone paramedic's cell phone with a questioning look.

He handed it over immediately. "Of course, sir."

Karim's chief of security came on the line after the first ring.

"How did they get in? I want a report the second you find something," he told the man in Arabic. "I want the whole building in lockdown until everyone inside is verified. And I want a digital copy of the security tapes e-mailed to me immediately."

"Yes, sir."

He handed the phone back and focused on the foreign woman who was watching him with morbid fascination. She looked even more impossibly beautiful than his first impression had been—high cheekbones, delicate features, eyes the golden brown color of a perfectly ripe, sweet fig. Eyes that held wariness and secrets, and a certain amount of plucky determination.

Then it clicked.

Media.

A less disciplined man would have groaned. She probably wanted an interview for some foreign paper. Sheer bad luck that she had caught him at a moment like this. There'd be no way now to keep the attack out of the papers. She'd be impossible to shake off. But he had other things to do, which meant he had to get her—and the distractions she brought—out of his life as fast as possible.

"At which hotel are you staying?"

She drew a deep breath and pulled her spine straight. "I need to talk to you first. I'm looking for Aziz."

His fists clenched. He made a point to relax them. Not a reporter then. Aziz. Of course. He should have known.

Aziz had always been the lucky one between the two of them, the ladies' man, or as some Western tabloids had once called him, the Playboy Sheik. Aziz had been in his element at the high-society events of Cannes and Monaco, and had kept a party house—with Hollywood celebrity neighbors—in Miami on Star Island. He'd lived the high life and pursued a wide range of interests, had dabbled in everything from yacht racing to desert archaeology.

"And who are you?" he asked.

"Julia Gardner." She extended her hand. Some of her color had come back. Her skin was now the palest of pinks. A tangle of bead bracelets encircled her slim wrist.

He didn't move.

She pulled back immediately. "I didn't mean to offend you. Sorry. Force of habit. I have trouble remembering all these strange rules." She snapped her full mouth shut. That lasted only a second. "Not that I think your country is strange. Just strange to me. *New*. New to me. I—"

"No offense taken."

"You look just like your brother." The words spurted from her before she pressed her full lips together once again.

His mood darkened. Maybe at one point Aziz and he had looked alike—they were identical twins. But nobody had dared compare them for a long time now, not since a childhood accident had taken the sight of Karim's right eye, leaving a hideous scar on his face. "You knew Aziz well?"

She glanced away.

So, Julia Gardner, too, had some trouble looking at his face, despite her earlier bravado. He resisted the impulse to shift into his usual half turn.

"We met when he was in Baltimore a couple of months ago," she was saying. "I haven't been able to reach him and I came here and— Look, I just want to talk to him. The man at the front desk told me I should ask you." She kept her hands clasped together tightly in her lap, but her shoulders were drawn straight and tall.

"Aziz is gone." The muscles in his jaw pulled tight. The pictures that flashed into his mind brought raw pain every time. He'd been closer to his twin brother than to anyone else in the world. The hot rage over the unfairness of Aziz's death hadn't diminished any in the month since his funeral. Nor had Karim's desire to seek revenge.

The corners of her eyes crinkled with worry, which

she tried to mask with a nonchalant smile. "When is he coming back?"

He forced air into his constricting lungs. "We had a well explosion last month."

He could see when she understood finally. Shock and pain flashed through her eyes. She stood, agitated, a hand pressed to her stomach, then opened her full, lush mouth, but no words came out. Color drained from her face all over again. She swayed.

He caught her and helped her fold to the gurney.

"She fainted, sir." The paramedic who sat in the corner, trying his best to remain invisible and give them privacy, moved forward and managed to clip a monitor on her index finger without actually touching her. Her vital signs showed on the small screen behind him.

Fainted. Karim blinked and let her go, stepped away from her. He didn't have time for this. He didn't have time for her. Period.

He would absolutely *not* allow her to sully Aziz's memory with scandal. He was fairly certain about why she was here. She wasn't the first. Others had come looking for Aziz after his international trips. They wanted to keep the party going, have access to Aziz's wealth and a shot at becoming one of oil-rich Beharrain's latest princesses.

She was too late. He watched her. Miss Gardner might not know it yet, but she was leaving on the next plane out of the country.

It seemed perversely insane that he was actually looking forward to going a few rounds with her before her stubborn nature would accept that decision.

He was ready to give her his ultimatum, but she still didn't stir.

His annoyance with her switched to concern. She did look vulnerable, her skin losing color again, all that hair tangled around her. She looked like an angel, injured after falling to earth. "What's wrong with her?"

He preferred that stubborn chin of hers thrust forward, as she faced him down, even if she were here to cause trouble.

He wouldn't let her.

"Could be from the stress or heat exhaustion. She's probably not used to our climate." The paramedic was administering an IV, again with the absolute minimum of touching. Then he drew blood into several vials. "If we went to the hospital, they could do tests as soon as we got there."

Karim rested his gaze on her face. She hadn't wanted to go to the hospital, had been pretty adamant about it. And he'd told her he wouldn't take her there. "Call ahead and have Dr. Jinan meet us at my house. You can take the blood to the hospital and call over when the results are ready."

He was about to take the troublesome angel home. He ignored the voice in his head that said he would probably live to regret his decision.

Julia woke in a strange bed in a strange and ridiculously opulent room, with a strange woman peering over her. An IV bag was attached to her arm. She panicked for a second, her gaze darting around. Her hand slid to her abdomen under the cover. No pain there. "What happened to me?"

"Hi, I'm Dr. Jinan." The woman smiled. She wore a gold-threaded, deep blue *abaya,* no veil. Her startlingly sharp eyes, which were lined with kohl, fixed on Julia. "You were near an explosion and fainted afterward."

Disjointed memories rushed her, and Julia pulled the silk cover higher on her body. The dark red fabric was as resplendent as the rest of her accommodations. "Where am I?"

"You are a guest of Sheik Karim Abdullah in his Tihrin palace. You're fine. You have a good, strong pulse. Once this IV runs out, we can remove the needle. Feeling better?"

"Thank you. Yes." She sat up to prove it. She didn't like the idea of some strange doctor examining her while she'd been unconscious. She didn't want anyone to know her secret.

"Did you have enough to eat and drink today?" the doctor asked.

Julia noticed the platter of food on a low, round table behind the woman—fresh fruits and other bite-size nourishment that looked exotically unidentifiable, but not the least bit appetizing at the moment. These days she was alternating between ravenous and nauseous, and was currently feeling the latter.

"Yes, thank you." She drew a deep breath to dispel the queasiness around her middle.

"Please do remember plenty of fluids. Our summers are mercilessly hot. I hope this little incident won't ruin your enjoyment of our beautiful country." The doctor smiled, all mothering warmth. "Looks like the IV is done. Let me take care of that." She removed the needle without causing any pain, stuck a cotton ball over the puncture wound. "Bend your elbow and hold this here for a few minutes."

She stood and began placing everything into her old-fashioned, black leather doctor's bag. "I'll be back to check on you tomorrow. Try to get as much rest as possible until then."

"Thank you, but that won't be necessary." With Aziz gone, she had no reason to stay in the country. "I will be leaving here."

Dr. Jinan gave her a smile one would give a petulant child. She was poised and self-assured, obviously a woman secure in her own power, challenging Julia's preconception of the women of Beharrain. Every rule had a few exceptions, she supposed.

Not that she had time to ponder the doctor. Karim Abdullah walked in immediately, as if he'd been waiting outside. He paused at the door and exchanged a few words with Dr. Jinan.

Julia searched their faces, unable to figure out anything. They spoke in Arabic. Did they know? They couldn't. Nobody could tell just by looking at her that she was pregnant, not even a doctor, she was pretty sure of that.

She would have told Aziz her secret. Probably. That was why she had come here. He was the father and he deserved to know, even though he had cut off communications with her. Or so she had thought. Now she knew the truth about why he hadn't returned her calls. The shock was still as fresh as it had been when she'd first heard the news.

Pain filled her chest and squeezed her lungs. Aziz was gone. It seemed impossible. She had never known anyone as filled with life and wide-open to the world, as charming.

He'd charmed a great many people; she had found that out when she ran a search on him on the Internet after he'd returned to his home, and she'd seriously considered taking him up on his invitation to visit him. The celebrity reports were full of his pictures, labeling him the Playboy Sheik. That had been a disappointment, not that he had promised her anything. The information had been enough to make her realize the brief affair for what it was: a few days of fun with an exotic stranger. She'd succeeded in putting Aziz out of her mind until those two pink lines appeared on a white plastic stick.

She took a few days to digest the news. Then called him without success. If she'd checked the Internet again, she would have found out about his death…wouldn't have come here…to his daunting brother.

A few of those news reports she'd read mentioned Aziz's twin. They had called him the Dark Sheik, without explanation, making her wonder. And now she was in the Dark Sheik's house. She looked around. *Scratch that*. The Dark Sheik's palace. God, it sounded like a gothic novel.

She had figured she would come here, would see how Aziz felt about the possibility of a baby. She wasn't going to tell him until she got a better idea of what kind of man he really was. Their time in Baltimore had been way too short. They had had some whirlwind dates and one night of passion, the day before he left. She had thought herself to be half in love with him and had been sure he felt the same. She was pretty certain now that he hadn't, but still, he was the father, and she had wanted to give it another go, if for no other reason than so she could tell her child later in life that she had tried. Her own parents had been all messed up. If she could help it, she wanted something better for her baby.

She was going to come here and see how Aziz was in his own environment. When and if she felt comfortable with it, she would have told him her news. Not a moment before that. Whatever happened, she was going to protect her baby. She was never going to let her or him go.

"Doctor Jinan tells me you are well." Karim came over once the woman left. He was not handsome, not with that scar. But he had a strong, masculine presence that drew her full attention to him. He stopped at a respectable distance from the bed, looking larger and harder than Aziz, infinitely more dangerous. Where Aziz's face had reflected humor, mischief and a sexy sort of cockiness about life, Karim's was bathed in darkness. And she didn't think all of that came from his scar.

He was wearing a fresh, crisp suit, his hair neatly combed. She felt dirty and sweaty and rumpled in comparison, but wouldn't let that stop her.

"Thank you for your hospitality, Mr. Abdullah." Grateful that nobody had undressed her, she pushed off the cover and swung her legs over the side of the bed, glancing around for her shoes. *There.* She slipped into them. "I'm sorry for all the inconvenience I caused."

With Aziz gone, she had no intention of staying here a day longer, no intention of letting Aziz's family know about the baby. Maybe it wasn't the right thing to do, but she was leery of the culture and felt none too trusting toward Aziz's twin brother. He looked as if he could—and would—take the law into his own hands if he felt the need. And he was a sheik, son of a king, as Aziz had been. He probably had a fair amount of power.

When her child was eighteen, she would reveal the truth and leave the decision up to her or him.

"Would it be possible to call a taxi?" She flashed Karim her most polite smile, refusing to be intimidated by him.

Given her social and economic background, she'd spent half her life being intimidated by the wealthy and powerful, by people in charge. But she'd had to get over that in a hurry when she had joined a nonprofit organization and had to interact daily with the elite. And over time, she'd learned that they were just like everybody else, with the same joys and fears and virtues and weaknesses.

Not that she could see Karim having a whole lot of fears or weaknesses. He had faced that car bomb down, cool as anything, and the memory of the incident was still making her heart beat faster.

"May I ask what your plans are?" He had his hands in his pockets as he rested his dark gaze on her. He might as well have been carved of solid rock, he looked that unmovable. But he was quick—she remembered him diving for her from his car. He loomed larger than life.

Exactly the kind of man she needed to avoid at all cost. She swallowed to wet her mouth.

"I'm going back to the hotel and probably flying out tonight if I can change my flight. I'm truly sorry about your brother." She was, and she needed time to deal with the sudden news. But she needed to get away from Karim Abdullah's searching gaze first.

"Perhaps you could tell me why you were looking for him?" His voice was even and low, with the sort of tone that made it clear he wasn't a man to mess with.

She'd gotten that message already.

"We were friends. I thought I'd stop by to see him. You know, long time no see. A chance to catch up. That sort of thing." She flashed him another winning smile.

He watched her as if he could see right through her, and she didn't appreciate how nervous he made her. It had nothing to do with the four-inch scar that made him look like a desert warrior despite his elegant suit. The overwhelming sense of power that emanated from him was what she was leery of.

"Thank you for your hospitality." She got to her feet and stepped around him, half expecting him to stop her.

He didn't. "Were you going to tell Aziz that you are carrying his child?"

She was halfway across the room, but the words stopped her more effectively than anything else could have. She was too scared to turn around and look at him, afraid of what he might read in her face.

"I'm not—"

"The paramedic took your blood in the ambulance. The hospital called with the results," he said in an icy tone. "You're not the first woman to come looking for him after one of his foreign escapades. I assume you're here for money?"

She winced, because that came uncomfortably close to the truth. "It's not Aziz's child," she lied. She would manage on her own somehow. She didn't want this dark sheik to have any kind of hold on her.

"My thoughts precisely, but I'd just as soon be sure. I want the case closed once and for all. I hope you won't mind a DNA test when the child is born."

She'd be long back in the U.S. by then, protected by U.S. law. They couldn't take her baby away at that point, even if they could find her, which she would make sure they couldn't.

"No, of course not." She schooled her face and chanced a look at him.

His expression remained unreadable, only his eyes darkened further, if that was possible. "Good. I hope you'll like your rooms. I'll introduce you to the staff this afternoon. You can pick your personal maid then."

The air got stuck in her lungs as she stared at him, startled. Was he completely nuts? "I'm not staying." She wanted to be very clear on that.

He paused for a moment. "That's a good strategy. Reverse psychology." He inclined his head with a small smile. "I give you this, you seem smarter than the others. But whether you prefer to stay or go has no bearing on anything. Your child might be the grandson of a king, and as such, one of the heirs to the Beharrainian throne." He watched her closely.

She felt the blood drain from her face. She'd known that Aziz was one of the king's cousins. But she knew they hadn't had a close relationship. And the king had a son. She hadn't taken succession into account. It wasn't something someone in her life and position thought much about.

"I'm sure you already considered that," he went on. "I hope you won't be disappointed to hear that a child, even if proven to be Aziz's son, would not be at the front of the line of succession. But in the line nevertheless. You must understand that I cannot allow you to leave the country until the bloodline is determined. Our very law would forbid it, except with the permission of the father. Aziz is gone. As his brother, I'm responsible for you and your baby."

If ever a sentence had the power to stop her heart, this was it. She was getting sucked in, losing control, the very thing she'd been most afraid of. She shouldn't have come here.

"This is insane. I have nothing to do with you. You can't keep me here. I'm an American citizen." She backed toward the door, relaxing marginally when he stayed where he was.

"You will find that in Beharrain, Beharrainian laws are given a priority over ideals of foreign countries thousands of miles away."

Was there a hint of threat in his steely voice?

She kept moving, but he still didn't follow. Not even when she reached the hallway and ran to the left, not knowing which way the exit was, but wanting to get away from him and the nightmare this trip was turning into.

Before long she'd reached a palatial marble foyer. The front door was open, but there were armed guards at the wrought-iron gate that led to the street.

"Excuse me," she said when they wouldn't move out of her way. Maybe they didn't speak English.

Step aside. Please, step aside. She wanted to get out before Karim decided to come after her. She didn't think he would let her go this easily. She glanced behind her, then back at the men who looked as unmovable as the seven-foot-tall brick walls that surrounded the property.

"I need to leave," she said slower and louder, knowing that was unlikely to make a difference. "Please." She pointed toward the gate. They had to know what she wanted.

"You are to leave the palace only in the company of Sheik Abdullah," one of them said after a moment, without looking at her.

So the language barrier wasn't an issue.

Her breath caught. Desperation rose inside her—desperation, fear and anger. She shouldn't have come. She had thought she would be able to keep her child safe while giving her or him the kind of large family she never had. But she understood now that wasn't possible. To keep her baby safe and with her meant that she had to escape far, far away from here. She would *never* give up control of her baby.

There had to be a way. She refused to accept that she, along with her unborn child, was a prisoner in a foreign land, held at the will of the Dark Sheik.

Chapter Two

She was fighting a losing battle. Sheik Karim Abullah's palace was better guarded than the Pentagon. But Julia wasn't the type to give up.

Since she had resigned herself to the fact that she wouldn't be able to escape on the ground level, she went up, sneaking through the night. She wasn't sure what she was hoping for, perhaps a large tree that came near one of the balconies. Trying something—anything—had to be better than sitting in her gilded prison of a room and crying her eyes out like she had done for the first half of the night.

She hated how weepy her overactive mommy hormones made her. This was not the time to give in to weakness. But she was emotionally exhausted and ravenously hungry. Hungry to the point that she was afraid her growling stomach would be heard.

She stole down the second-floor hallway, pausing in front of the first door. She pushed it open a fraction of an inch at a time and glanced around the lavishly appointed living room she discovered. Some sort of a suite. Other doors opened from here. The furniture was exquisitely made—all ornately carved wood—and was breathtaking even without her being able to make out the true colors of the luxurious fabrics in the moonlight.

Her gaze settled on a phone on a small, octagonal table. Her U.S. cell phone didn't work here and there wasn't a phone in her room. She wished she knew the number of the U.S. embassy by heart, and dialed zero, hoping to get directory assistance. Nothing happened.

She tried zero-zero, her stomach continuing to growl. No ringing on the other end. Zero-one. Just one. One-one. A disembodied voice said something in Arabic then the line went dead again. She gritted her teeth with frustration and took a banana from the fruit bowl next to the phone. An apple's crunching might give her away. She peeled it then bit in, and nearly moaned at the soft sweetness that diffused on her tongue. Heaven.

Her food tray had been removed that afternoon on her request when the smell of food had made her nauseous. She had refused dinner on principle—not the smartest thing, in hindsight.

She grabbed another banana and was stuffing it down the front of her shirt when a small noise came from behind one of the doors opposite her. She froze, nearly ran, but stopped herself. She needed to find a balcony, a way out.

She picked a door that was half-open, figuring she would make the least noise that way, and found herself in a large bedroom. The space was dominated by a sprawling bed, draped in black sheets, that didn't look slept in. A handful of papers lay tossed on the night-stand, next to a book.

Then her gaze was drawn to the source of the noise she'd heard before. A bathroom off the bedroom, lights on, the water running. She was facing a full-size, gilded mirror on the bathroom wall that was angled away from her. The picture it presented made her mouth go dry and her feet freeze to the tile floor. She swallowed the chunk of fruit in her mouth with some trouble.

Karim stood in an open shower with black mosaic tile and one of those drenching, foot-wide showerheads, water sluicing down his tanned skin. He stood with his back to her, so she had an unobstructed view of the scars that ran down his back, breaking up the otherwise perfect lines of the most incredible male body she had ever seen. He had his hands up, bracing himself on the wall, his head hanging as if deep in thought, tension evident in his corded muscles.

Shadows stretched across his back. She couldn't tell from this distance whether they were scars or some sort of tribal markings.

Another person might have looked vulnerable naked, but not the Dark Sheik. Strength radiated off him, and danger.

He reached to the side and turned off the water with one sinuous movement.

Okay, so Mr. I'm-Lord-of-All-I-Survey was sexy. Very. She couldn't care less. She was leaving. Now.

He wrapped a black towel around his waist then

turned, his dark gaze finding hers unerringly in the mirror. He didn't show surprise. Somehow he'd known she'd be there, staring.

How humiliating.

"Is there anything you wanted from me, Julia?" His voice was low and measured, full of innuendo and contempt.

She wanted to turn and run, but his gaze wouldn't release her. When he strode closer, she backed away without looking where she was going, hoping she was backing out the door. Instead, in a few steps, her back bumped against the wall.

He was a short foot from her, looming dangerous in the semidarkness of the room, his wide shoulders outlined in the light that came from the bathroom. Drops of water glistened on his dark skin. He smelled like soap and sandalwood. He was the most erotic and intimidating sight she'd ever seen.

"Looking for a substitute sheik for your plan?" He put his right hand to the wall next to her head. His hand being higher than his shoulder, droplets of water ran backward, along his carved granite biceps.

Her heart jumped to her throat. He thought she'd come here to seduce him. She moved the other way, but that arm came down, too, and boxed her in. She didn't feel panicked as much as mesmerized. Blinked her eyes. *Snap out of it.* How dare he?

"Don't touch me." She shoved with her free hand, indignation giving her strength. She tried not to notice the hard muscles of his warm—and still wet—chest under her fingers. Her limbs were shaky. From exhaustion, no doubt. She was likely still jet-lagged, too.

He didn't budge a millimeter, but a dark eyebrow slid up his forehead. "Changed your mind? Scare you, do I?"

Maybe. Okay, more so with every passing moment. He was large and powerful and utterly overwhelming after a hellish day. She was well aware that he could kill her, and with his title and station in the country, there probably wouldn't even be a questioning.

Tears threatened to fill her eyes. She gritted her teeth and held them back. This was not the time for a hormonal moment. "Go to hell." She lifted her head and stuck her chin out. "You want to intimidate me? Congratulations, you succeeded. That's what turns people like you on, isn't it? Scared women."

A muscle jumped in his face, just beneath the four-inch scar on the right side that started above the eye socket and ran straight down. And then she realized the eye didn't move along with the other one. He was blind on that side. Not that his left eye wasn't lethal enough on its own.

He took his time to look her over from her bare feet to the top of her head, returning to linger on her breasts, which had grown already during the pregnancy and were stupidly sensitive to smoldering looks from half-naked men. More misery to blame on hormones.

"The same things turn me on as any other healthy man, I suppose," he said, his voice a notch lower than before.

The space between them was insanely small. Without warning, the adrenaline that had been pumping through her already was metamorphosing into primal heat, making her fingertips tingle.

He had masculine lips, what some old-fashioned novels might have defined as cruel. Heathcliff lips. Incredibly sexy. She got a little woozy from looking at them this close.

The sharp sense of desire was insane, but perhaps understandable, considering that her body was hormonally unbalanced and out of her control.

His voice was a soft whisper when he spoke. "Why are you here, Julia? Why are you in my bedroom in the middle of the night?" He lowered his head as if wanting to carefully listen to her response.

If he came any closer, he was going to feel the banana she'd hid down the front of her shirt.

Her pulse sped, and not just from the danger of being discovered as a fruit thief. "Looking for a glass of water," she croaked out with effort. Her mouth did feel extraordinarily dry. She looked into his good eye.

His Heathcliff mouth tightened, but he didn't back away an inch. "Excuses?" He examined her. "Interesting. You're bold enough to come to me like this, yet you feel the need to come up with a pretext for seeking my bed."

Outrage quickly overcame awakening desire. Of all the conceited— "You know what I'm doing?" she asked sharply, and ducked to the right from the circle of his arms. "I was trying to get out of this stupid place. You have no right to keep me here. This is kidnapping." She darted toward the door.

If she thought the lack of sight in the right eye was a weakness, she was quickly disabused of the notion. He caught her easily.

"You will stay for as long as I see necessary," he said. "If I catch you trying to run—I've given you some freedom, Julia. Freedom that can be taken away."

What freedom? Her room? Meaning he could be keeping her closer to him? How close? His bed sprawled imposingly in her peripheral vision. She didn't want to know. Or maybe he'd meant he had some dungeons in the basement. That would be more likely. Nothing would have surprised her at this point.

Fear spiked her pulse. "I was wrong," she told him with all the contempt she felt. "You are nothing like your brother."

"And what do you know about Aziz?" His gaze slid to her abdomen. "My brother wasn't an irresponsible man."

A moment passed before she understood what he meant.

"He wasn't." And that was all she was prepared to say on the subject of birth control, which obviously was not as reliable as she'd thought.

His gaze journeyed back up, slowly, to her face.

The warning system in her brain was screaming that she should run for her life. "This baby has nothing to do with you and your family." She was desperate to escape his palace.

He didn't respond.

"You don't believe me."

More silence, just his dark gaze searching her face.

"And if I said the child *was* Aziz's? Would you believe *that?*" she said, testing him.

"No."

"So you're determined to think me a liar." Which, God help her, she was quickly becoming. But yes, she would do even that. She would lie, cheat and very possibly kill for her unborn child.

The question was, how far was Karim Abdullah willing to go for his niece or nephew?

"I'm just questioning your motives," he said.

"Is that what you call it?" She braved a sneer. "In my country this would be called kidnapping."

His masculine lips pressed into a tight line.

Her heart drummed against her rib cage. She tugged her arm. "You have to let me go."

And this time, he released her at last. "Get some sleep. I made an appointment for you for tomorrow morning. You'll get the full workup. You had a fall today. I arranged for an ultrasound."

Not one for minding his own business, was he?

Her initial instinct was to protest, but she hadn't had an ultrasound yet. Her first was scheduled for the week after her planned return to the States. She desperately wanted to see her baby. And she was no longer sure when exactly she would be back in Baltimore. Or if she could afford even the most basic medical care.

She did have that fall. And despite feeling fine, she did worry. And it wasn't as if he was going to give her a choice about going. "Fine. But don't think you're coming with me. Absolutely not."

"And I looked into testing," he said. "There's something called amniocentesis that can be done during pregnancy. They can obtain DNA and determine paternity."

She didn't know how she felt about that. The test would prove that the father was Aziz. That would bind her even tighter to Karim, an outcome she wanted to avoid at all cost. Could she refuse? What would that gain her? *Time*.

She turned from him and marched out with the half-eaten banana in her hand, calling a "Go to hell" over her shoulder on principle.

As she sped her steps, the banana under her top dislodged and fell to the floor. She picked it up, glad he didn't see her. But a glance back at his bedroom door revealed that, in fact, he had.

He'd come after her and was leaning against the door frame, watching her with a superior smirk on his face. "You may take the whole fruit bowl if you'd like."

THE RADIOLOGIST asked him no questions, one of the privileges of being sheik. Karim stared at the staticky-looking black-and-white screen, at the blurry outline of what seemed like a head and part of the abdomen. He kept his gaze studiously on the screen, ignoring the creamy expanse of skin in his peripheral vision.

He had come in with her because despite the blood test, he still half believed there might not even be a baby. Tests could be wrong. Tests could be altered for the right amount of money. She could have had it all set up at the hospital.

And if she were pregnant, he had half hoped that the ultrasound would reveal that she was lying about the child being Aziz's. The time of conception could have been wrong. Or the kid could have had stark red hair and looked obviously Irish, or whatever. What did he know? He'd never seen an ultrasound before.

But the date of conception was right on the money, during the time that Aziz had been in Baltimore. And, although the gray blob on the screen bore no resemblance to Aziz, Karim could hardly hold that against it. It barely looked human.

But here was the funny part, the thing he hadn't seen coming: the longer he looked at the kid, the more he wanted to believe the woman who lay on the hospital bed with her eyes glued to the screen and tears misting her fine eyes.

"Nice, strong heartbeat. See that?" the radiologist asked him.

And he could. The heart pulsed rapidly in the middle of the screen. The image was mesmerizing. He didn't like the softening it brought out in him.

Most likely, the woman was a money-hungry scammer.

The report he had received on her last night certainly pointed in that direction. Her family had been anything but upstanding and responsible. Her father left early on. Her mother dumped her and her siblings into the foster-care system. Julia floundered around for a while after that, then went to college on some sort of government program. Ended up with a nonprofit organization where she seemed tolerably successful.

He considered her alluring beauty, the crown of hair that to his disappointment she wore up today, that light in her eyes as she stared at the screen.

Hell, who wouldn't have fallen for that? Maybe she'd done so well because she could flirt successful business-men into large donations. But her track record hadn't been enough. Her organization was downsizing and she was let go a month ago.

Pregnant and without any income. That had to be the definition of *desperate* for a woman.

Last night when he'd gotten the report, he'd been certain she was lying about the baby belonging to Aziz and was impatient for that DNA test. He wanted her to be gone.

Then she had come to his room, and in a moment of insanity, he just plain wanted her. He had wanted her to offer herself to him, and not only to prove him right about her character.

But now, looking at the child, the rapidly beating heart on the screen, suddenly he wanted there to be a baby from Aziz, someone left behind by his brother. He wanted the feisty, auburn-haired beauty to be true and not a conscienceless liar. He wanted her and her baby to belong to him.

Because of Aziz. He would take care of them for Aziz. There was so infuriatingly little he could do for his dead brother otherwise. Finding his killer was about it, which he would do even if he had to put his own life at risk in the process.

"Looks like you are just entering the second tri-mester. Everything looks well," the radiologist said. She was a petite, modest woman who wore a veil that covered most of her head and a large part of her hospital uniform. "The baby seems healthy."

"I called Dr. Jinan last night. She said something about the possibility of an amniocentesis," he said.

"That would be done sometime between week sixteen and week twenty of the pregnancy. Is there a concern about genetic problems?" The technician looked up.

"An issue with paternity," Karim growled, trying not to care that Julia flushed red with embarrassment.

"We don't normally do it for that purpose." The woman bowed her head.

"But it could provide confirmation?"

She nodded. "There are risks."

"What risks?" Julia asked.

"In a small percentage of the cases, the procedure can cause miscarriage. But if you absolutely have to—"

"No," he said at the same time as Julia, and hated the surprised look she gave him. Did it really stun her that much that he wouldn't put the baby's life at risk? "The procedure is not that necessary."

She would just have to stay around until the baby was born and they could do a no-risk DNA test. He would have to find a way to get her to agree. Despite his threats, he couldn't really hold her that long against her will, not in the current political climate. The country was trying hard to build strong diplomatic relations with the West, to prove that the place was safe for tourists and the culture prosperous and civilized. A rogue sheik kidnapping an American woman would definitely create damaging publicity.

She had come for money, he was pretty sure about that. All he needed was to figure out the price of her cooperation. They would discuss it over dinner tonight. He wasn't buying her burning need to leave, anyhow. Could be she was just being coy.

The prospect of her prolonged stay and the continued annoyance it was sure to bring should have bothered him but, oddly, it didn't. "So the child is healthy?"

"All looks as it should."

Dr. Jinan walked in and greeted them warmly, looked at the screen over the technician's head. "Everything is in order?"

"Perfect."

"Since you did have a fall, I'd recommend another day of rest. No work, no exercise, no sexual relations," Dr. Jinan was saying to Julia. "But if you continue to feel fine, you can resume all normal activity the day after tomorrow. If you have any problems, please don't hesitate to call." She gave Julia an encouraging smile.

Karim felt his shoulders relax, then tense again when his cell phone beeped. His chief of security. He turned off the ringer. He'd call the man back later. He didn't want to miss anything.

Never in a million years would he have expected to find himself in a place like this. He was resigned not to marry and have children of his own. He'd tried back in his early twenties. But he'd seen the look in the girls' eyes at the introductory meetings. The fathers were all willing. But he scared the women. And he didn't want to take a wife who would be repulsed by the sight of him, would cringe every time she looked at him for the rest of their lives.

Julia Gardner was scared of him, which didn't keep her from standing up to him, but she never once cringed.

"Can you tell if it's a boy or a girl?" The question was barely audible, her voice filled with wonder. Her face was radiant. A deep joy shone through her skin, joy that could not be faked.

He could not remember when he'd felt such unrestrained, undiminished happiness, if ever. She was about glowing with it, her beauty intensified until he could barely look away from her. Maybe a veil for her, too, wouldn't be a bad idea while she was in this country, although he didn't plan on letting her wander around without him being close behind.

"Not yet." The radiologist smiled. "Maybe in another month or so."

"Oh."

The child moved, looked like it was waving. Cute little bugger. Karim couldn't help a smile, but schooled his features back into place before Julia could notice.

If she realized that he was softening, who knew what outrageous demands she could make. If the child was Aziz's, Karim would take care of it, no question. If it wasn't… He looked at the woman who was still staring at the screen, teary-eyed. Something flipped over in his chest at the sight.

She was in a desperate situation. Had to be, to go into a far-flung scheme like this and try to pass her child off on a man who wasn't the father. He glanced at the screen again. If the DNA test came back proving Aziz had nothing to do with this, he could still see that she was able to raise the baby. Hell, he could afford it.

"Would you like some pictures?" the radiologist asked.

"I'm not sure." She glanced down. "I can't really pay for this."

"We'll take the pictures," Karim said.

"We can also make a copy of the video—"

"Send it to my palace."

She wouldn't look at him as the radiologist wiped off her flat belly, which he'd been trying to avoid taking notice of. Sure didn't look like new life was growing there. Maybe she wasn't eating enough. Something he would have to pay extra attention to.

She didn't talk to him until they were out of the examination room and going down the stairs. "Thank you. I don't have to thank you, because you kidnapped me and bullied me into this whole visit, but it was a moment, and…otherwise I would have been alone. Which probably would have been a step up from going with a kidnapper. But if I consider that you'll be my baby's uncle—"

"You're welcome." Did she always babble on when she was emotional?

She gave him a dirty look. "One more thing."

He drew up an eyebrow. Here we go. She was about to make her first demand.

"Please don't humiliate me in front of people like that again." Her words were issued softly.

Damned if he knew why he was feeling like a heartless bastard all of a sudden. His jaw muscles pulled tight. "Sorry." He didn't know which one of them was more surprised when the word was out.

"Wow, that sounded like it hurt. Was it your first time?" She grinned.

He glared back.

"You could just let me go," she said when they were in the car, the air conditioner going.

"Too cold?" he asked as he pulled into traffic.

"Are you kidding? I have a furnace inside. I could be standing on the snowfields of Siberia and be hot. Pregnant bodies produce lots of energy."

He hadn't considered that. "I can't let you go." He turned down the boulevard.

"You're a sheik. You can do anything you want."

She had an answer for everything, didn't she? Fine.

"I don't want to let you go," he said.

"Don't you ever watch international TV? Your views on life and responsibility are pretty archaic. You don't have to take care of me. I don't belong to you." As she said the last sentence, she enunciated each world deliberately.

"I don't have time for TV." He didn't bother addressing her wild notion of her not belonging to him. "I want you to write me a list of what you need. Both for you and the baby. And you need to eat more," he said just as a dark sedan cut off the car following them to get directly behind him. "I can bring a nutritionist on staff while you're with us."

He kept his attention on the sedan, his warning senses

perking up. The car was moving with too much purpose, the driver unnecessarily aggressive.

"I don't need a nutritionist. I eat healthy and I eat as much as I need. I won't be staying that long anyway."

She clearly resented his interference. And right now wasn't the time to discuss just how far he was willing to go to make sure her pregnancy went as smoothly as possible.

He looked at the rearview mirror again. "Listen, we might—" Too late, he saw the gun. He swerved. "Watch out!" He pushed her down just as the rear window exploded.

He heard the shards hit leather, but his seat and headrest protected him. A glance confirmed the same for Julia. He stepped on the gas and the car lurched around the minivan in front of them. But his attackers—two men, their faces obstructed by tribal-style headdresses—followed.

He swore under his breath. Should have brought his security along. But he didn't want anyone in his family or at the company to know about Julia Gardner and her claims yet. Didn't want to deal with the questions about him going to a women's clinic. If her story were untrue, he didn't want to unnecessarily tarnish Aziz's memory and bring his honor into question.

The car in front of him was slower than slow. For a moment, he swerved into upcoming traffic to get ahead, expecting Julia to scream at him. She didn't, but horns beeped all around them. He chanced a glance at her when he'd returned to the right side. She sat pale-faced, hanging on to her seat with a white-knuckled grip.

He snapped his attention back to the road in front of him. "We can handle them."

"We *can't* handle them. Oh, my God. Call the police!" She squeaked the last word.

"I'm a little busy." He growled under his breath, not at her, but at the men. By the time the police found them, this could be long over. Either he shook their attackers, and shook them fast, or one of their bullets would find its aim and end the chase.

He swore under his breath again. More stress was the last thing Julia needed in her condition. Not that he knew anything about her condition. But he would learn. For Aziz's child. *If*— Damn, but the uncertainty drove him crazy. He wasn't a patient man on his best day.

When they got out of here, he was going to get her to agree to stay in the country, then lock her up safely in his palace and not let her go until the baby was born. Maybe he would move to Aziz's place for the next six months. Living under the same roof with Julia might be more than he could handle. Especially if she kept sneaking into his bedroom. He was concerned about that as much as he wished for it.

"Hang on."

He was a good driver and put all his skills to use. For a moment or two, it seemed he might be able to put enough distance between his car and the assassins behind them.

Then a bicyclist, of all things, pulled in front of him, oblivious to danger. And he swerved, running the car up the cement rails of the shoulder, the right two tires leaving the ground. If they were to flip… He grabbed the steering wheel and maneuvered as best he could. He had to get the car back on the road. After an endless moment, he did manage.

"Are you all right?" He didn't dare take his eye off the road to look at Julia.

"I'm not all right. People are trying to kill me!" She sounded shaken. "What is it with everyone? Is everybody completely nuts around here? What are they thinking? Just go!"

He did, and for a moment was sure that they would make it. But the second bullet was more accurate than the first. The force of it slamming into his flesh smacked him against the steering wheel.

They were out in the open. The bullets kept coming. He had a woman and an unborn child to protect. Pain spread through him. He'd been hit. He couldn't tell how badly, and it was information he needed. All their lives depended on it.

Chapter Three

All his life he wanted to be a holy man. He had even changed his name to Mustafa, which meant *chosen*. And he indeed knew that Allah had chosen him when the only god trusted this most important task to him.

Old evil had returned into this world—old evil that offended the faith of his people and threatened their souls. He had sworn to destroy it and all who had come in contact with it, all who had been contaminated.

And the One God had been gracious and had given him followers, a tight sect of righteousness and light. They were all happy to die for the cause.

But so far, their work had been blessed and it had been Aziz Abdullah who had died. Mustafa smiled as he looked out over his garden. That first task had been done right. But they had much longer to go it seemed.

The evil objects had not been recovered. The world and his faith had not yet been saved. The idols had been passed on and contaminated yet another man: Karim Abdullah. But Karim, perhaps in his ignorance or already too tight in the grasp of the evil, did not realize that he needed to be purified.

It couldn't be helped. Mustafa stroked his beard and closed his eyes against the strengthening sun. His free hand held his cell phone. The call would come soon. Karim, the guardian of evil, would be dead.

Then, without a powerful guardian, the idols would be found. Yes. He smiled into the sun. He and his faithful followers would most certainly triumph.

"HOLD ON TO THE steering wheel," Karim said, pressing a hand to his wound, then pulling it away and looking at it, probably checking how badly he was bleeding.

Pretty badly. Then again, when it came to gunshot wounds, she wasn't sure there was such a thing as "good."

"The steering wheel," he said more urgently.

Julia stared at him. Was he crazy? Apparently, because he was letting go already, just expecting her to grab on as he pulled a gun—*a gun*—from under his suit jacket with his still-functioning right hand.

She had no idea that he'd been armed. She hadn't run around with armed men all that much before, smart girl that she'd been. Past tense, definitely. Everything that had been normal in her life had changed the second she'd set foot in Beharrain, and she was losing hope of being able to reclaim her old, sane life anytime soon.

First step was to stay alive.

She grabbed for the steering wheel as Karim twisted in his seat and returned fire.

Wow. Okay, guns were deafeningly loud when going off next to one's ear. You learned new things every day, she thought. Except all this, including how to evade armed pursuit, was stuff she didn't want to learn.

Insane. She really, really shouldn't have come here. This was another world. She didn't belong. She might not even survive it. Anger welled inside her, at her own stupidity for having come, and at the man next to her who could have let her go the night before, but hadn't. She could be back in Baltimore by now. At that moment, she hated Karim with the same fierceness that she hated the situation she was in.

"You know, if you didn't go around kidnapping people and bullying them into doing whatever you want, maybe everyone wouldn't be trying to kill you!" She might have been yelling a little. She was a smidgen on the stressed side.

He squeezed off another shot. "Everyone isn't trying to kill me. These are probably the same people who put the bomb in the car yesterday."

"That's comforting. I take it all back then," she snapped. "Could you *please* turn back to the road?"

She glanced nervously at the stick shift. As long as he kept the speed steady, they were fine. But if they had to slow for anything, she had no idea what to do with it.

Not that slowing seemed to be in his immediate plans. He was pushing the gas pedal nearly to the bottom, making maneuvering difficult to the extreme. He'd almost flipped them a few minutes ago, and she had a feeling he might succeed yet. Another experience she would have preferred to leave out if it was all the same to the gun-happy sheik next to her.

He shot another round, then—miracle of miracles—did as she asked and took back the wheel. He floored the gas and was able to gain a little more distance between them and the car that followed.

"You could drop me off here. Anywhere."

He didn't bother with a response.

They zoomed by the entrance of the boulevard that his palace was on.

"Obviously, you have some problem areas in your life." She looked behind them pointedly. The attackers were now three cars behind. "Maybe if you dealt with those, you'd have less time to meddle in the lives of others."

"I don't meddle. Stop nagging." He executed another maneuver.

"I don't nag. Where are we going?"

He frowned as if he hadn't considered that. Okay, to be fair, he'd been kept pretty busy with getting shot and all.

"They'll expect me to go back home and might head us off," he said.

"MMPOIL?" There was security at the company. She'd seen a number of guards while asking around for Aziz.

"I don't want to bring this fight to a building full of my employees. They—" he jerked his head to indicate the men who followed them "—might expect that, too. They've probably been following me long enough to know any place I could go. Wherever I go, someone might be there waiting."

Death was waiting for them all around. Not a happy thought. *Don't panic. Breathe.*

Her gaze fell on her purse in her lap, settling on the magnetic room cards visible in the front pocket. "We could go to my hotel." An idea was forming slowly in her mind. She needed to get away, and not just from the men who were shooting at them, but away from it *all*. Her brain worked furiously at one possible solution.

He seemed to be considering her suggestion, looking in the rearview mirror. "The Hilton downtown." He nodded.

So he knew where she'd been staying. Obviously, he had checked her out. What else had he found? It didn't matter. The important thing was that he was going along with her idea.

He took the next exit and was there in minutes. They had been closer than she'd thought, not knowing the city. The sparkling high-rises, all glass and steel, were testaments to modern architecture, mixed in with ancient mosques and minarets. The sight was breathtaking but foreign, and she got disoriented too easily. The day before, after careful instruction from the concierge, she'd only been able to find MMPOIL after three tries, going around in circles for over half an hour.

In hindsight, it would have been better if she hadn't found the place and Sheik Karim Abdullah at all.

"Do you have a card for the underground parking?" He cast a sideways glance at her as he pulled up to the gate.

She fished out her parking pass and handed it over to him. The gate opened. They were in. Her plan might work yet. Her number-one objective was to keep her baby safe. To achieve that, she would do whatever was necessary. And since being around Karim was the opposite of safe, what she needed was to get away from him.

Keep cool. Keep thinking. Give nothing away.

He glanced into the rearview mirror one more time before shutting off the motor and tugging off his blood-soaked jacket. His tie came next. He tried to wrap it around the wound. She got out and walked around to help him, doing her best not to look at all the blood as she pulled the silk tight.

Another scar, she thought, and was beginning to wonder just exactly what sort of life the Dark Sheik lived. She had a feeling she didn't want to know. Had Aziz been like this when he was at home? Somehow she couldn't picture it. She tied off the length of silk.

Karim didn't wince. "Thank you."

She stepped back. "It doesn't mean I forgive you. I just don't want to have to explain to my baby later why I let his uncle bleed to death." He was lucky that family was so important to her.

The corner of his mouth twitched, which annoyed her. She hadn't been trying to be funny. She meant every word she'd said.

He pulled the jacket back on, its dark fabric hiding most of the bloodstains. Not that it mattered in the end. They were lucky enough to make it to her room without running in to anyone, although the elevator ride was a tad tense on the way up.

"I'm going to wash this off so I can see the damage."

He lifted his left arm and headed for the bathroom as soon as they were inside the room and the door locked behind them.

The hotel was furnished and decorated in Middle Eastern style, rich fabrics and colors, copper tables, a multitude of pillows everywhere. The room looked as if it had been decked out with the treasures of old-time caravans. She'd been dazzled when she had arrived, but barely noticed the exotic interior now. Of course, a hotel room was never going to impress her again after having seen Karim's palace.

She sank onto her bed, which had been made since she'd left it the morning before, the starch going out of her all of a sudden. God, that car chase had been petrifying. She folded her hands over her abdomen and breathed deeply for a few seconds, gathered herself as best she could, until she felt a little better. She had not, in fact, come to harm so far, and neither had her baby. That was the most important thing.

With Karim being out of the room, even if he did leave the bathroom door open, she could almost pretend that everything was back to normal, like before she'd started out on her ill-fated trip the previous day. Except she wasn't big on pretending.

Her mother had pretended all her life and look where that got them. She'd pretended that she didn't have a drinking problem. She'd pretended that her marriage was just fine, up until the day her husband had walked away. Then she pretended that she could start over if she just got rid of her daughters, abandoning them to foster care.

You didn't face reality, your life fell apart real fast. It was a lesson Julia learned early on. She was a firm believer in confronting problems head-on. Which was why she had come to Beharrain in the first place. To face down her issues with Aziz, gain some sort of a resolution, then go home.

Instead, she'd been kidnapped by an overbearing sheik, held against her will overnight and nearly killed. *Twice.*

But Karim hadn't hurt her, had made sure she and her baby were okay. He had paid for a full checkup and an ultrasound. With video. She almost regretted that she would be leaving him before that came in. At least she had the pictures in her purse.

Time to make her move.

She pulled the nightstand door open and lifted out her travel kit, found the leaf of small, white sleeping pills. She kept them in the kit because she never slept well when traveling, but she hadn't dared take them on this trip. She didn't want to do anything that might harm the baby.

She popped a pill into her palm, then after some thought, popped a second, then a third. He was large and strong. She didn't want to make the mistake of underestimating him. She put the kit away, grabbed a glass and filled it from the bottle of bubbly mineral water on the table, then broke the tablets up, sprinkling them into the water. When she was done, she swirled the water around. The bubbles hid the rapidly dissolving chunks.

"I don't think the bullet hit anything serious. It went through muscle." Karim was coming from the bathroom.

He startled her so badly that she almost spilled his drink.

"Here. You lost blood. You should have some fluids." She handed him the glass, feeling only a twinge of guilt. None of this would really harm him. He'd have a good sleep, which would help him heal. He'd be upset when he woke and found her gone, but he would just have to get over it. "Let me tighten the bandage."

He'd used the tie again, but it looked loose, the best he could manage with one hand.

"Thank you." He drained his glass while she fiddled with the length of dark silk and held her breath.

"What are we going to do next?" It was a miracle that she wasn't trembling with nerves. As soon as he passed out, she was out of here. Her rental car was still at MMPOIL, so she would call a cab to take her to the airport. She was determined to be on the next flight out of the country. He'd taken her passport the night before, but she'd seen him put it into his wallet, which had to be in his suit jacket. She shouldn't have any trouble getting it back.

"The baby looked good," he said out of the blue. "You were satisfied with the doctors? If not, I can ask for others."

"They were fine." The medical personnel all kow-towed to them. They barely dared to look Karim in the eye. "I'm sure they'll do their best. They're all scared to death of you," she said pointedly.

"Aren't you?" He held her gaze.

"No." At least not in the physical sense. "I must be stupid," she mumbled to herself as she turned away.

"Don't say that."

"I came here." Case in point.

"You did the honorable thing. I respect that."

"Enough to let me go?" She felt another pang of guilt for drugging him.

He smiled. "No."

The moment passed.

He walked to the window and looked out, flipped open his cell phone and talked at length with someone in Arabic.

"Who was that?" she asked when he hung up and walked over to sit in the armchair by the desk.

He looked mellow. So far she'd seen him with his usual controlling expression, angry and scowling. Mellow was definitely new. Actually, it didn't look all that bad on him.

"My security." He closed his eyes for a second. "I told them to look out for anyone suspicious both at work and at home. I gave them a description of the car that followed us."

She didn't have time to ponder his looks. "Tired?"

He shrugged it off. "Tell me how you met my brother."

God, she so did not want to get into this now. But she had to do something while she waited for the drug to work. Maybe talking him to sleep wasn't such a bad idea.

"He was at a fund-raiser dinner I organized."

He nodded. "My brother lived a busy social life when abroad. Fund-raiser for what?"

"Summer camp for kids in foster care. For siblings. For the most, the system tries to place siblings together, but it can't always be done. I worked for an organization that tries to make sure that these brothers and sisters stay in touch. This way, when they get out of the system, there's a relative out there that they had contact with over the years. Sometimes the older ones can help the younger ones. We try to give them that sense of family."

She thought of her two sisters whose memory was faded and spotty. She could recall specific incidents and conversations, but the faces were becoming blurry. Finding them had been the first thing she'd tried to do when she had left foster care at eighteen. She had failed so far. Back then, records hadn't been computerized. The agency that had placed her family had been flooded out several times, many of their files destroyed.

She had managed to find her mother, but she had passed on by that time.

"You still work there?" he asked. His eyes were becoming hazy, but his gaze on her face was unwavering.

She looked away. "You lost blood. Do you want me to call an ambulance?" Suddenly she was worried that three pills might have been too much. Maybe he did need help. She could call and be gone by the time they got here. He did have that handy-dandy company ambulance at the ready, after all.

"I'll go in later and have the wound cleaned and sewn up. I want to get you someplace safe first."

Protecting her seemed to be a reflex with him. She wondered if he was like this with everyone.

"I'm safe here." They weren't going anywhere together.

He closed his eyes for another moment. "I asked for some of the security staff to come over. They should be here soon enough. Maybe I'll have them take you to Tariq's place, my other brother. His wife is American. Did Aziz tell you that?"

She shook her head. Oh, God, his security was coming?

"That's right." He looked increasingly absentminded. "Aziz hadn't met Sara." His face darkened. He leaned back in the chair. "I think I lost more blood than I thought." He pulled his gun and laid it across his lap.

"That's okay. Take a minute to rest."

She'd given him the pills ten minutes ago. They usually worked on her in about that time. And she'd given him a triple dose.

"So your organization doesn't miss you while you're here?" He didn't seem to be easily distracted.

"I'm no longer with them. They had to cut back. Some of our top corporate sponsors left. With the economic downturn, our donors haven't been able to support us like before, either. Aziz was brought by a friend of a friend." God, he probably thought that she'd just latched on to his brother for the money. "He was really interested. He thought the summer camps were a great idea. I didn't—"

"Take advantage of him?" He finished the sentence for her.

"If you're going to imply that I only slept with him to get more money…" She glared at him, knowing that her hormones made her more emotional these days, but not caring. So she was touchy lately, so what? She'd spent the last three months nauseous and tired to death, feeling as if she'd been beaten over the head.

"Did you?" he asked without emotion.

"No!"

He simply nodded. Blinked. "My brother supported a dozen charities, both Beharrainian and international."

He had to pass out before his security got here. It was her only chance. *Please, please, please,* she prayed silently, watching him for signs of fatigue without being too obvious about it.

He shook his head as if to shake himself up. "So you are currently unemployed."

She didn't bother denying it, just nodded.

"I take it you are here for money." He didn't look angry, just resigned. Yet another new look for him.

"I didn't come for money."

He arched a dark eyebrow.

"Not just that. It's not like that. I wanted to do the right thing. I wanted to tell him."

"But you would have been content going back without telling *me?*"

She should have. She should have run the moment she'd laid eyes on Karim. "I was afraid of how you would react. I didn't want anyone to assert any kind of claim over my child. I wasn't crazy about the idea of possibly getting kidnapped and held against my will." She glared at him.

His lips twitched. "Think of it as being my honored guest."

"Think of it as illegal," she retorted, wishing that he would pass out already. She was about ready to jump out of her skin.

"You could enjoy it. It could be a few months of vacation and pampering. It's not like you have anything to go back to."

Ouch. He was right, but she didn't have to like it. His assessment of her life sounded dismayingly pitiful. "You could let it go," she said. "What if I have a new boyfriend back home?"

He leaned forward, somewhat unsteady, and narrowed his dark gaze. He looked decidedly unhappy about the possibility. "Do you?"

She shook her head, didn't see any point in lying.

Her admission seemed to relax him. He leaned back into the chair again. His hands hung by his sides, his suit coat falling open. She shouldn't have any trouble getting into his inner pocket and fishing out his wallet. She would get her passport and borrow enough money so she could get to the airport. She so wasn't going to feel guilty about that. He had confiscated her purse. If she was driven to desperate measures, he had only himself to blame.

Oh, God, please, let him fall asleep. "Listen, I—" She fell silent when somebody knocked on the door. Despair surrounded her. How could they be here already?

He came to his feet, lurching forward unsteadily.

"Julia—" Then understanding flashed across his ragged face. "Julia?" This time he growled her name. The mellow phase was clearly over. He gave her a fierce scowl. Then he folded back into the chair, and finally passed out.

Oh, God. There would be hell to pay for this if they ever met again, which she would do her best to avoid.

His security was here. The scene would just have to be played out. She could stay right by the door when his men came in. With luck, they'd be focused on what was going on with their precious sheik and she would have a second or two to dart out.

The Hilton was an international hotel. There were other Americans here. She'd heard them downstairs over breakfast before she'd headed over to MMPOIL the day before. Once she reached the hallway, she would run like a champion and raise holy hell. She was prepared to scream her head off and bring all the other guests and the staff running. Even if the staff wouldn't take her side against a sheik, she was certain that her compatriots would defend her. If it was the only way to get out of this country and back home to safety, she wasn't averse to causing an international incident. She had few illusions about Sheik Karim Abdullah getting into any trouble.

She took a deep breath, ready for her escape, her hand on the lock by the time she thought to look through the peephole.

Two men stood outside, dressed in white robes and headdresses. One scanned the hallway, while the other was focusing on the door. They wore identical grim expressions. They didn't belong to Karim's security. She recognized them from earlier and the breath got stuck in her throat. It couldn't be true. This couldn't be happening.

"Karim?" Desperation made her voice high and squeaky.

She glanced back at him. His eyes floated open for

a moment before closing again. He looked formidable even slack-jawed.

She looked out the peephole again, her heart racing at double speed at the sight. The men waiting to get in were from that dark sedan that chased them, the same men who had done their best to kill Karim and her just a little while ago.

"Karim, you have to wake up." She judged the distance between her and the gun on Karim's lap, wondered if she could even figure out how to take off the safety. But before she could make up her mind, it became apparent that she wasn't going to have time to go for a weapon.

Something scraped against the card reader. She shoved her full weight against the door. That didn't seem as effective as she had hoped. She gained maybe two seconds. The security chain held the men back for another two. Before she could blink, they were already pushing their way inside.

Chapter Four

When the two men outside heaved and slammed the door open, Julia was smacked against the wall, the air leaving her lungs with a whoosh, pain exploding in her back. And she was glad that the point of impact hadn't been any lower.

She slid to the dark gray carpet that covered the floor, stunned for a moment, but pulling her hands in a protective gesture in front of her. *The baby. Don't let them harm the baby*. And it seemed, at least for the moment, that her prayer was answered, because the intruders paid scant attention to her.

One closed the door and guarded it while the other dove for Karim, shouting something in Arabic. Both men held their guns on him.

Everything was happening too fast, her mind reeling. The attack had come so unexpectedly, she couldn't catch up, couldn't think, didn't know what to do. She glanced toward the door, but she couldn't work up the nerve to tackle the guy blocking it.

At least Karim was rising to the occasion, lurching to the left, toward the bed. He squeezed off a shot but missed. His movements were definitely uncoordinated. He looked like those big game-reserve lions on the National Geographic Channel after being hit with the tranquilizer shot, ready to be tagged. Then he was on the floor, and for a moment she thought he had passed out and fallen, not realizing until he rolled under the bed that the drop had been deliberate.

Not that hiding out under there was an option. The attackers filled the mattress with lead the next second.

"No!" The word tore from Julia's throat unbidden. He was a controlling bastard, but she didn't want him harmed. Didn't want to be responsible for his death. She had given him the pills. She had immobilized him and served him up to his enemies.

He was her baby's uncle. He didn't deserve this. He was bossy and arrogant, but in some ways he was okay. Misguided as his efforts were, he did want to keep her safe. Just before the men came, he'd been talking about getting her to safety. And she had done this to him.

"No, please," she pleaded again, against the instinct to keep quiet and invisible, but the two bad guys didn't even glance at her.

The gunfire did stop, however. The guy who guarded the door stepped forward. The other moved closer to the bed and dropped to his knees in front of it, probably to check if their job was finished.

The air stopped halfway to her lungs. Karim was dead. And she would be next.

Whoever these two were, they wouldn't want to leave a witness. They just assassinated a sheik. She had no idea why and she didn't need to know right now. Their reasons were immaterial at the moment.

She had to do something. But she was frozen with fear, paralyzed by the smell of gunpowder in the air and by the sight of those guns and the assassins who held them. A terrible realization held her in place, the knowledge that there was nothing she could do to change the outcome of the situation she was in. It had been determined the moment the two thugs had busted into the room, armed against a drugged sheik and a defenseless woman.

Her hands moved protectively to her abdomen. She wanted the best for her baby, had promised the best, had sworn to provide the safety, love and family that she hadn't been given. She hated to fail even before her child was born. That was the thought that got to her more than anything, more than the possibility of Karim's death or her own. She could not face the fact that her child would never see the world.

Then something shifted inside her. To hell with the bastards. She was no defenseless woman. She was a mother. Nobody was going to hurt her baby.

She shifted and had the element of surprise on her side when she kicked at the gun in the nearest man's hand, kicked and met her aim, sending the weapon flying across the room. Almost at the same time, a gun went off, drawing her attention to the bed just in time to watch the other attacker fold to the floor, red blooming on his white caftan.

Karim rolled out from under the bed, his weapon in hand, but his movements were slow, his gaze unfocused. The remaining attacker took advantage and dove for his firearm, then fired as soon as he had it.

Karim's gaze finally caught on her for a split second before he put himself between her and the bullets. "Go!"

She didn't need to be told twice. Adrenaline pushed her to her feet. She got the door open, glancing back only to see Karim lunge after her as more gunshots exploded behind them. His momentum carried him another couple of yards before he slowed again, shook his head as if to clear his mind.

A million thoughts raced through her head in a fraction of a second, the topmost being that she was out of the room, could leave him now and he could do nothing to stop her. The guy with the gun wanted Karim. Karim would probably put up a fight, even if it would only last seconds, minutes at best. But it was time she could use. She could get away, be free.

Free. The word pounded through her head.

She would be free and Karim would be dead.

"Help! Please help!" she screamed toward the row of doors on each side.

Nobody stirred, nobody volunteered to rush to the rescue. Given the gunfire, the other guests were probably locking themselves in their rooms. Housekeeping was obviously working another floor. Not that they could have defended her against bullets with a broom.

She grabbed Karim's hand and dragged him toward the staircase. The fireproof steel door was just closing behind them when bullets pinged off the metal on the other side. She couldn't leave Karim behind. She would get him out of here, then leave him somewhere by the side of the road where he'd be safe. *Safer,* at least.

She shoved him forward then yanked on the fire hose and tied the door shut before going after Karim, who was tumbling down the stairs. She ran, grabbed his arm, and her momentum carried the both of them forward. He grunted and she did, too, along with him. He was heavy and not fully in control of his powerful body, hard to direct.

At the landing he slammed against the wall, leaving a bloodstain on the white paint. His arm was bleeding, but she didn't have time to worry about whether that was the old wound or a new one. Maybe she could put him out by a hospital, although, God help her, she had no idea where one of those would be in this city. "Go, go, go!"

The gunshots stopped outside the staircase, which meant the attacker was probably taking the elevator to cut them off. Julia raced for her life, muscles pitted against machinery.

The flight to the parking garage passed in a blur. She hadn't noticed before, but Karim had parked his car right in front of the door of the emergency exit, right where they came out of the staircase. Probably on purpose. He seemed like the type of guy who planned ahead.

He was now together enough to reach into his pocket. He opened the car with his remote, then handed her the keys.

Oh, God.

Of course, he couldn't drive in his condition. She hadn't even considered that. Which left her to handle the task. But she didn't know the city. And she was a mediocre driver at best, not equipped for armed pursuit. But she had no choice.

When he just stood there in drug-induced stupor, she dragged him toward the passenger side and shoved him in unceremoniously, slammed the door behind him before sprinting to her side. Then she remembered the stick shift. Why, oh why?

"I can only drive automatic," she yelled at him as if it was all his fault.

What were the pedals? Clutch, break, gas, if she remembered correctly. A high school boyfriend had spent some time coaching her on his pickup a million years ago, but it had turned out to be a brief relationship and she hadn't paid much attention to the driving lessons in any case, not when they were just a distraction between make-out sessions.

And make-out sessions they were, nothing more. She'd been a good girl all through high school, petrified that she'd get pregnant and would end up alone with a child. Her number-one goal had been avoiding becoming like her mother. She'd never slept with a man unless they were in a committed relationship, of which she'd had two. Then came those few irresponsible days with Aziz. And they had used protection. Not that it mattered. Fate sure had a way of laughing in her face.

She was going to have a baby.

If she stayed alive long enough.

Through some miracle, she managed to put the car in first gear. Karim had backed into his parking spot, so at least she didn't have to worry about backing out. Okay, which way? Most of the signs were in Arabic. She almost cried in relief when she spotted an old-fashioned English exit sign, a lit red box with white letters. Thank God for international hotel chains.

The first gear took her to the exit just fine. Then she stalled when trying to shift to second. She needed to start up the damn car all over again. She winced as the engine whined. She'd never driven a car this nice before, a silver BMW with more power than she was comfortable with. She really didn't want to break it. Then she thought, to hell with it, Karim's fancy car was the least of their problems.

She didn't dare look in the rearview mirror to see if the bad guy was behind them or not. She focused her full attention on the shift and clutch.

The shot Karim fired through the back window and the responding gunfire the next second tipped her off to the severity of their situation. They were sitting ducks unless she managed to get the car moving.

She got it into first gear again and moved up to the gate that opened on its own, no card required to get out. Thank God, because she had no idea where her parking pass was at this stage. She passed through and stepped on the gas, and with some grinding of the gears switched the transmission into second. They were out on the boulevard at last.

"Clutch. Shift. Now," Karim instructed.

Third gear slid into place with nothing but a small hiccup. Fourth. *Good, really good.*

Except that someone cut in front of her and she needed to slow, but knew that shifting down would make her stall all over again. She kept her foot steady on the gas pedal instead, and yanked the steering wheel to the right, going around the car in front of her, causing a minor disturbance on the road, and a flurry of beeping horns.

But the car was still moving. *Yippee.*

If her lips weren't frozen in a tight line of concentration, she might have smiled. The small burst of relief vanished soon enough.

"Where are we going?" She weaved through traffic, taking unnecessary chances just to keep a steady pace so she wouldn't have to shift.

He took a long time to answer. "Aziz's palace. Left at the next light, right, then left again." A long pause followed. "Blue." Was he still talking about the palace?

She caught a green light, thankfully, sailing through, barely slowing to make the turn. The tires squealed in protest. "Which right, the next right?"

When no response came, she risked taking her eyes off the road for a split second to glance at him. Karim slumped in his seat, completely out of it. She wasn't sure whether from the drug or blood loss. A hospital would have been great right about now, but they were clearly in a residential neighborhood.

And she had a feeling these residents were anything but ordinary. A row of palaces lined the road on each side, some traditional, some startlingly modern. She had to shift down. After some hesitation, she actually succeeded. Then she took stock of the front yards that were protected by stone walls and wrought-iron gates. There was no way she could just pull into a driveway and pretend to belong there. Especially not with the back window of Karim's BMW being blown out.

She glanced into the rearview mirror, but couldn't tell if they were being followed. She couldn't see the dark sedan anywhere, but that didn't mean the assassin hadn't commandeered another car. Assassin or assassins. She wasn't sure how badly Karim had hurt the one he'd shot. Could be they were both still out there, on their tail.

"Karim?" She reached over to shake him, couldn't be too forceful with his bad arm. "You need to wake up now."

The street she was on looked completely unfamiliar to her, all the signs on the buildings in Arabic. *Blue,* he had said. About every third house was blue.

He didn't seem to care. His head tilted to the side. For the moment, he was completely out.

She was lost in a strange place, her only possible protection injured and unconscious and there was a better than good chance that they had an assassin or two following not far behind—serious bad guys whom she was too inexperienced and frazzled to even hope to spot.

If things were going to get any worse, she didn't want to know it.

KARIM STRUGGLED to open his eyes, struggled to remember where he was. Through a slit, he caught a glimpse of Julia next to him, her hair all messed up and wild, her eyes wide as she stared at the road ahead, her face pinched in concentration.

They were in danger, but he couldn't remember why or from whom. He had to stay awake. Frustration pulsed through him, but he couldn't sustain the urgency of it. He felt like he was diving, underwater, floating in the deep. His body seemed incredibly relaxed. All was peaceful inside. He could sense turmoil outside, but felt as if it had been somehow walled off from him.

He smiled at the mermaid in the driver's seat. "You're beautiful." He slurred the words.

She barely spared him a glance. "Which house? You need to tell me which house it is."

Where were they going? He could only think that someone was after them and they must get away. But he couldn't keep focused on that for more than a second. "You shine like an angel."

"Speak English," she snapped.

Julia Gardner was an exceedingly beautiful woman. He liked her hair the most. And her eyes. Her skin glowed pink. Her lips were—

"Karim," she snapped at him again. "I need you to tell me how to get there."

Where were they heading? A long moment passed before he could remember. "Aziz."

"Right. Which one is his palace?" She sounded exceedingly impatient. Might have even growled a little.

The sound made him smile.

With effort, he turned his gaze from her and realized that they were on Aziz's street. He reached for the remote in his glove compartment, feeling darkness closing in. "Aziz," he said one more time, then sunk into oblivion.

"KARIM, WAKE UP! Wake up, dammit."

Julia took her right hand off the steering wheel, a move she could hardly afford, and shook him.

Nothing.

She grabbed the remote from his hand. What was this for? She pushed the top button. Down the road lined by modern palaces, a wrought-iron gate opened. She hoped there was a correlation between that and the remote. In any case, she had to get off the road. She had to hide.

Of course, the second she tried to shift down, she stalled the car. *Damn. Okay. Let's start over.*

First gear. Good. It got her through the gate.

She pushed buttons randomly until the gate closed and the door to a garage bay opened. Then she pulled in, gawking at the selection of sport and luxury vehicles. She closed the garage door. The lights came on automatically.

She sat motionless and listened, but could hear no car stopping in front of the house, no bullets hitting the garage door behind them. A reprieve. She leaned back in her seat and closed her eyes, wanting to stay that way forever.

But she had to get out of here, away from Karim before he came to. A glance at him confirmed that he wasn't even close to that yet.

She stepped out of the car, shaking from the chase and maybe a little with hunger. Something red caught her eye in the side mirror and she realized her clothes were bloody. From Karim. She had to find something to wear before she went out onto the street. A disguise wouldn't have been a bad idea, in any case. Just so the assassins wouldn't recognize her if they ran into each other. She needed one of those *burqas* local women wore, the black dress that made them virtually indistinguishable from each other.

A week ago she would have sworn that nothing and nobody could make her wear one of those things. Two days in this country and she was already begging to put on the veil.

Could be there was something like that in Aziz's palace. Not a *burqa,* specifically—he'd told her he wasn't married and none of his sisters lived with him—but even a black sheet would do. Karim had black sheets—the brief flashback to when she'd been in his bedroom raised her core temperature a few degrees so she pushed that particular memory away.

So she was a little attracted to him. So what? He was an attractive man. Tall and wide-shouldered. That scar of his only made him look fiercer. But he wasn't for her. For one, he was Aziz's brother. That made it all strange somehow. Plus, by tomorrow this time, she'd be home.

The only contact she planned to have with Karim was when she helped her child write letters to his uncle in a couple of years. Family was important. She was going to allow contact, she'd decided at one point. Making her daughter or son wait eighteen years for the truth didn't seem right. But she was going to take precautions. She didn't see going on vacations together in their future.

She cast a glance at him. He was sleeping, the dashboard propping up his head, in what looked like an extremely uncomfortable position. He seemed a little less intimidating in this pose. She pulled the key from the ignition and looked at the key ring. If Karim had the remote to Aziz's gate, it stood to reason that he would also have the key to Aziz's house.

She could help him in and make him comfortable. Could look at his wound and, if needed, even call for help if she found a phone book and the number for the ambulance. If she could figure out the listing in Arabic. Hopefully there was a symbol of a red cross or something along those lines next to it. In a country where illiteracy was a major problem, surely they would think of something like that.

She would find herself something to cover up with, call an ambulance and book it out of here before anyone arrived. Seemed like the perfect plan.

She walked around, dragged him out of the car and stood him upright. He wasn't completely unconscious, not so much that he was dead weight. But his movements needed firm direction and a lot of encouragement. She nudged him to the stairs, propping him against the wall while she tried the keys one by one. She hit the jackpot on the sixth try, went into some sort of an entrance room, swore at the blinking red light on the state-of-the-art security system—a flat-screen monitor built into the wall.

Of course, a palace would be secured. She was lucky she wasn't sitting neck deep in Rottweilers and security guards.

"Wake up. We need the code." She shook Karim, inhaling the pleasant, citrus smell of the palace, noting the white marble tiles under her feet. "Karim. You need to wake up. Hello."

Nothing.

The security system beeped once.

She took that as a warning and tentatively touched her hand to the screen. A window appeared with a fingerprint drawing on it. She reached for his hand and pressed his thumb against the spot. He didn't resist. Another window appeared with a blinking cursor. Probably waiting for a password.

"Wake up!" She pried his good eye open with her fingertips. Only the vacant look spoiled the gorgeous sable color. "What's the code?"

He shook his head and tried to focus on her without success. She was beginning to feel real guilty for doing this to him. Then hardened her heart. If he had listened to reason, she wouldn't have had to take things so far.

"The code." She turned him toward the screen. Him being bossy was annoying, but having him completely helpless wasn't all that fun, either.

He gathered himself and lifted his hand, punched in a series of numbers she didn't quite see as she had to hold him up. But she did see when the light switched to green.

"Thank you." She leaned him against the wall and let

him go, closing the door behind them. Mission accomplished. She was practically on her way to freedom.

A small beep sounded again. By the time she turned around, he was sitting on the floor with his back resting against the wall and his eyes closed. The security light was red once more. He had rearmed the system.

And just like that, she was trapped again.

"FAILURE WILL not be accepted. This is a holy mission. Do not come back," Mustafa yelled into the phone before remembering that his men needed encouragement as well as discipline. He switched to a more fatherly tone. "You will find them. Your path will be guided by righteousness."

So there had been setbacks. He knew he was merely being tested. He was prepared to show the strength of his faith by never giving up, never letting an unexpected problem get the better of him.

He'd lost a man. A noble sacrifice.

Every cause had martyrs. The loss would only strengthen him and his small group of true believers. They were all prepared to die for what was true and right.

You fought against the devil, you had to expect that there would be casualties. He had expected that a few men would have to be sacrificed. He was willing to give that to the cause. In truth, he was willing to give so much more.

His calling was to rid the world of evil, and he was prepared to do that, whatever the cost. But some of his followers were untrained yet, their minds not as strong as they should be. They didn't see losing one of their own as glorious as he did. They would learn. Teaching them was part of his responsibilities, a sacred duty entrusted to him.

But his enemies were multiplying, it seemed. Who was the woman? A whore no doubt. No woman of honor would spend the night at a strange man's house, nor would she take him back to her hotel room with her. If he had any doubts about whether Karim stood on the side of righteousness or darkness, that alone would have revealed the truth. Karim had been infected by evil, his actions turning immoral already. Who knew what he would do if Mustafa didn't stop him?

He felt the full weight of that responsibility. He would not lay down his burden until his task was done, his mission completed.

"Check our primary points. I will also send out the others," he told the man on the other end of the line.

His team had been following Karim around for weeks now. They knew all the places he regularly visited. He was wounded; he would want someplace familiar to hide, someplace he felt safe.

Little did he know that for a man who sided with evil, there was no safe place among righteous believers.

Chapter Five

If she left now, the alarm would go off. Julia could see it all: a foreign woman running into the street with blood on her clothes and a palace security siren blaring behind her. If they caught her, if they found Karim, a bleeding, semi-conscious sheik... She would be tossed in jail quicker than she could say, "I want to call the American embassy."

She didn't want to stay here with Karim, but she didn't cherish the thought of a Middle Eastern women's prison, either, or the chance of running into the assassin or assassins on the street. She would see to Karim's injuries then think of something, she decided, and headed off to find some water and some strips of clean linen. She called a "Stay where you are" over her shoulder, knowing it to be unnecessary.

The first thing she registered when she opened the door that lead to the rest of the palace was that the place was a complete mess. Drawers overturned, furniture pulled away from the walls, books and clothes scattered all over the place.

But even through the mess, the splendor of the palace was obvious. It had been built in a more modern style than Karim's, with a lot of straight, clean lines and a certain amount of masculine severity. Everything was the best money could buy: the marble, the crystals, the furniture and the electronics equipment that was the latest on the luxury market.

She found a bathroom, used it then washed her hands thoroughly with soap, looked for something to collect water in, but couldn't find anything. She moved on, hoping to find a first-aid kit. Then realized that the place was too enormous to search from top to bottom just now and settled for a clean white towel.

On the way back, she picked up a priceless-looking modern art vase and filled that with water in the bathroom.

Karim was still completely out, coming to only when she began removing his clothes. His jacket was bloody all over. Guilt pricked her again over drugging him.

"Sorry. It seemed like a good idea at the time."

Then again, if he hadn't tried to stop her from going home, she wouldn't have had to resort to such desperate measures. She focused on the task ahead.

"I'm going to try to figure out what your injuries are, see if any of them are life-threatening." If he could on some level comprehend what was going on, she wanted him to know that she was removing his clothes for a perfectly valid reason.

She tried not to pay too much attention to the strong column of his neck as she unbuttoned his shirt, barely gawked at his wide shoulders, tanned skin, the muscles of his chest and his arms. He was perfectly built, perfectly proportioned, his body all masculine grace and beauty. Not that she was impressed or anything.

She did her best to think of Steve, the weasel who'd broken her heart. She'd thought they'd been in a committed relationship for the past five years. She'd made it clear that all she wanted was marriage and kids, the stability and warmth of a family. And Steve had strung her along, promising all that, but always asking for just a little more time before they got started. Then he moved to L.A. and left her behind like he left his old job and old apartment. He needed to reinvent himself, he'd said.

And then along came Aziz, who treated her like a princess and charmed her so thoroughly her head was spinning. He'd promised nothing and at that point, she appreciated the honesty and, on the rebound, couldn't resist the man. She knew it had been a mistake as soon as the short fling was over. It hadn't fixed anything, hadn't made her any happier.

Then she'd found out that she was carrying his child.

She was petrified that she wouldn't be able to care for a child on her own, like her mother had been unable to care for hers. But not for a moment did she regret this baby.

"That should do it," she said when she had Karim stripped to the waist. She couldn't picture Karim wooing a woman with outrageous gestures. "I bet you're the strong, silent type."

He gave no indication of hearing her. He actually was

softly snoring. Good news, that. Seemed he was just asleep and not unconscious from blood loss.

She wet the towel and began washing him with it. A bullet wound and a couple of grazes. She did her best to scrub away the dried blood, leaving only the area of the bullet hole untouched. That was a deep wound that thankfully stopped bleeding. She didn't want to chance opening it up. He didn't need to lose any more blood. She wished she could find a phone book and figure out the number for an ambulance.

"I hope you won't get an infection this quickly. When you wake up you can call that doctor. You'll be fine."

She bandaged his wounds and left them alone.

She needed more cloth and more clean water to wash him completely clean. There was dried blood on most of his torso. When she was done with the front, she leaned him forward carefully to look at his back. And gasped at the angry scars that marred his skin, a horrific testament to his past.

She couldn't image what could have happened to him. Whatever it was, it seemed a miracle that he had survived. She cleaned off the blood, not so much of it here. Then tentatively dragged a finger over the largest scar, feeling the rough edge that ran down his skin.

She might have been overwhelmed by the dangers of the last two days, but it was clear that Karim Abdullah was no stranger to violence.

She pulled away, resolving again to get away from him at the earliest possibility. But first, she might as well make him a little more comfortable.

KARIM LET HIMSELF sink into the most pleasant dream he'd had in a long time. A woman's soft fingers were caressing his skin. Her touch was as smooth as the finest Arabian coffee and took away the pain that burned his arm.

Her voice was warm and sweet like a honeyed treat he was particularly fond of. Her scent of jasmine and vanilla invaded his senses. Her fingers ran down his chest. The dream disappeared for a while then came back again. She was touching his back now, very gently. He was aware it was a dream, even as he dreamt it. No woman would want to touch his scars, no woman would willingly look at them. But he pushed reality away and pulled the dream closer, not wanting to let go the sweet comfort of it.

The dream faded again and other images came. Pain. People dragged him over cold, hard ground. He was a child now, kidnapped and beaten when he had tried to run. The men who dragged him talked openly of killing him, of dividing the price his own stepbrother put on his head. But they decided to beat him first to pass the time and to teach him a lesson for having tried to escape. They used a camel whip to peel the skin from his back.

But that light, feminine touch brought his dreams back from the dark past. Slim fingers placed a cold cloth on his forehead and washed his face. A soft torso pressed against his midriff as the woman leaned over him.

And as sleep wore off, his body awakened. Instincts warred. A part of him warned of danger. Another part wanted to forget about everything else and take all that softness that moved around him. Jasmine and vanilla. Arousal washed over him as he woke, and a sudden awareness. On reflex, he caught the slim wrist that had been the first thing he saw, a hand rising above him. Then he rolled, pinning the woman under him.

In the next second two things registered: the pulsing pain in his arms, and that the person looking at him wide-eyed was Julia Gardner, the woman who possibly carried his brother's child. *Off-limits.*

But just now, his brain still slow from drugs and sleep, he couldn't deny that he wanted her, wanted her with a fierce need he hadn't experienced in a long time.

The room was shrouded in semidarkness. Dusk was settling outside. She hadn't turned on the light. Smart. Her intelligence had never been in question. Her stubbornness was the thing that had gotten her in trouble.

He pulled away and sat up, his mouth as dry as the *Rub Alkali,* the Empty Quarter, the deadest part of the desert. His limbs were still weaker than he would have liked, his movements not completely steady.

Memories of the hotel room and the attack flooded back. "You poisoned me." The words came out on a rasp of outrage. He cleared his throat.

Her eyes grew huge for a second, then she looked down, away from him and backed up a few more steps.

He glanced around. They were at Aziz's palace. "How did we get here?" His memory had some serious gaps when it came to the last couple of hours.

"I drove. You gave directions. Sort of."

He reached up to his arm, to the bandage. So she had

helped. Tried to kill him then changed her mind? "What have you done?"

She moved farther away. She wore a pair of men's linen pants and tunic, the soft material clinging to her figure, the straight front of the shirt stretching over her full breasts. The sight did nothing to dampen the arousal left behind by his dreams, arousal that he tried hard to ignore. Apparently, it was possible to be spitting mad at someone and want her at the same time. A damn inconvenient situation.

"I'm not going to be your prisoner." She raised her chin and looked him square in the eye at last.

"And you're prepared to kill me to get away?" He pinned her with a hard look. "Because it is my duty to protect you on my brother's behalf. A duty I will not betray."

"I didn't poison you. I was trying to put you to sleep long enough to get away from you."

"You rendered me useless before my enemies." He kept his anger in check. Barely a touch of it showed in his carefully controlled voice.

"And if the tables were turned? How would you feel if *I* kidnapped *you?*" She used typical women's logic.

But the suggestion did inspire a brief fantasy. He shook his head to clear it. He was a man. Their situation could not be compared. He didn't need protection.

He had, when he was a child, he thought then. And felt again that sense of hopelessness and desperation, the stark fear of his childhood. He hadn't had that dream in a long time. It brought back some dark memories. But it also made him understand a little why she wouldn't like the feeling of helplessness, the idea that her fate was in someone else's hands.

"You are not my prisoner. You will not come to any harm." He hoped to set her at ease. She had to accept her fate and stop trying to fight him, putting both of their lives at risk.

"You're protecting me? I was just fine before I met you. Since—" She sputtered with indignation.

"You have a sharp tongue and a strong will that is most unbecoming in a woman." He felt it his duty to point it out. But he couldn't truly mind. She was something to behold when she got all worked up. Those fine eyes of hers came alive with sparks, energy vibrated off her in waves.

"It's a miracle I'm not dead yet," she snapped and made a frustrated gesture.

Her slim hands reminded him of another part of his dreams, and made him realize that at least some of them had to be true. She had undressed him and cleaned him, bandaged his wound.

"If you want me safe, let me go," she said with some vehemence.

"Those men wanted *me*." His statement didn't negate the fact that she had been in real danger. In that parking lot with the car exploding, on the road when they'd been pursued, at the hotel. A problem he needed to solve. Without letting her go. That was nonnegotiable. "What happened has nothing to do with you. Wrong place, wrong time."

"So I would have been only collateral damage. That's a comfort." She gave him the evil eye. "You have no right to keep me here."

Really, she was pushing him too far. "You have no right to decide the fate of a prince of Beharrain. I will make sure that you are safe. I will make sure that you and the baby are well and get the best possible medical care."

She pressed her tempting lips together.

Good. Maybe she'd be quiet and stop fighting him. He needed to deal with other things. Later, after he had a chance to think over this latest attack, after he had taken the appropriate security measures to deal with the obvious step-up in the attacks against him, he would set aside some time and figure out what she would need from him to consider staying. Be it money or any other advantage, he was willing to give it.

He reached for his cell phone, but it wasn't in his pocket. It must have fallen out during the fight at the hotel. Plenty of phones in the palace. He called his head of security, filled him in on the developments, set up a meeting for the morning. They should be all right here for the night. He wanted to stay put until the drug wore off completely. His enemies didn't know he was here. If they did, they would have come after him already. No sense in giving his location away by ordering his men to his side.

When he was done with the call, he checked the bullet wound and decided not to call a doctor to the palace, either. At the moment, aside from his closest people, he didn't trust anyone. He started for Aziz's safari kit that contained every tool for every possible emergency, but stopped in his tracks when he opened the door that led from their room to the rest of the palace.

"What have you done here?" It seemed impossible a single person could cause so much damage in such short a time, but he was starting to learn that Julia Gardner was no ordinary woman.

"The place was like this when we got here," she said defensively.

He shot her a skeptical look. But as he moved farther inside, he realized she was telling the truth. Some of the heavy furniture that had been pushed away from the walls she couldn't have possibly moved alone.

"Looks like someone broke in here." He wondered how long ago. He hadn't been out to Aziz's place in a week since he'd paid off the servants, sent them away and closed the palace down.

"They took some paintings and other valuables. But they didn't find what they were looking for." He walked through the great meeting hall where low, overstuffed chairs and a modern take on the traditional oval, Arab coffee table occupied the middle of the room.

"How do you know?" She came up behind him.

"If they came for money, they could have taken a lot more things." The amber chandeliers alone were worth a fortune. "They were searching for something." He indicated all the overturned furniture. In one place, they'd even chiseled up the marble tile. "They didn't find it and got angry, caused some damage to blow off steam." He pointed at the smashed ebony chest. "Then they grabbed a couple of things so their operation wouldn't be a complete waste."

"What were they looking for?" She moved forward and scrutinized the scene. She was definitely not the type of person to quietly sit in a corner while someone else took care of any problems at hand.

He surveyed the room for a long moment. "If we can find that out, we might be able to find out who they are."

"The same people who want you dead?" She followed him as he walked through the palace, surveying the damage and looking for clues.

He couldn't not be aware of the graceful way she walked, of her feminine presence beside him.

"Most likely." He stopped and took in the stubborn look in her eyes. He had to be crazy for even considering telling her the truth. He had figured he would protect her from that. But Julia Gardner seemed dead-set against accepting any sort of protection.

He hesitated for another long moment. Glanced around one more time, just to delay. They were in the kitchen. Expensive china was scattered on the tile floor. Signs of violence were all around them. Maybe it would be better if she weren't completely ignorant of the how and why. "Take a seat."

She walked to one of the many boxes the servants had packed, and opened it.

He had a feeling she'd do the opposite of what he asked just to spite him, no matter how reasonable a request he put to her. "Suit yourself." He shrugged off his annoyance.

She pulled out some canned food and puzzled over the flowing Arabic script that must have looked like scribble writing to her. "Do you cook?"

He raised an eyebrow.

"Forget it." She mumbled something about rich people and their private chefs.

"I haven't told you everything about Aziz."

Her eyes snapped to his face. She dropped the can back into the box. He had her full attention now.

A shadow crossed his heart. "I have reason to believe that Aziz was killed. I've been working on tracking down the men responsible for his death."

Her face went white. He watched as the fight went out of her, replaced by stunned denial.

"Why would anyone want to hurt someone like Aziz?" She paled another shade.

He stepped closer and put a steadying hand under her elbow, cursing himself for being so aware of the fact that he was half-naked and her clothes hid little of her charms. Jasmine and vanilla. He tried not to breathe. He really was a better man than this, wanting blindly what wasn't his.

She had made it clear that she wanted to be as far from him as possible and was willing to risk her life to get there. The thought stung, so he pushed it away. But could not push away the awareness of how soft her skin felt in his palm.

He was relieved when she pulled away to sit.

"And now the same people want to kill you. Why?" She looked up at him, bewildered.

"You wanted to kill me," he pointed out, smiling at the irony.

"I wanted you asleep. So I could escape." She asserted her previous claims once again, and he was tempted to believe her.

"You drugged me unconscious when we had two assassins on our trail." In his book, that came pretty close to wanting him dead. "What did you think was going to happen when they caught up with us?"

If possible, she turned whiter. "I didn't realize. I—" She fell silent and braced her elbows on her knees, leaned forward to bury her face in her hands.

Her hair was undone, tumbling over her shoulders, cascading to shield her face. She looked lost and fragile just then, bringing out all his protective instincts until he reminded himself that she was more than capable of handling herself. She had rendered him helpless, something his enemies hadn't been able to do.

And yet, she hadn't left. Something to think about.

"You changed your mind. You didn't leave me to them. Why?"

She murmured something like, "I must be too stupid to live."

If anything, she was too smart for her own good, certainly for his. He watched her for a long moment before making up his mind. "You did it for honor," he said. "Because you are an honorable woman, you will do what you must. You dislike me, but you protected me. So you have to understand then why I must protect you."

"Because you dislike me?" She glanced up.

She didn't need to know just how far that was from the truth. "Because honor demands it."

"I hate the whole concept of honor. It's frustrating." She drew herself straight in the chair. "And it's stupid."

"You might hate it, but you have it."

"Well, it's damn inconvenient."

He grinned at her. She was the only woman he knew to swear. He should have been shocked. But to be honest, he liked the starch in her. He could easily see why Aziz had been captivated by her strange personality.

Aziz.

Had she been the woman of Aziz's heart? Had Aziz planned to go back for her? He couldn't imagine any sane man not wanting to go back for her. For that matter, he couldn't imagine any sane man willing to leave a woman like Julia Gardner behind in the first place.

Perhaps he hadn't known his twin brother as well as he thought he had.

His mood turned dark as he left the kitchen and strode toward the back storage areas, not stopping until he found the safari kit, which had been riffled through, but not destroyed.

He pulled out a bottle of disinfectant and a sheet of butterfly bandages, some sterile gauze, and sat on the floor to take care of business.

"Let me help." Julia kneeled next to him.

And because he wanted to feel her touch on his skin again, despite his better judgment, he allowed her. He sat still as she unrolled the stained strip of linen and poured the disinfectant over the wound, didn't move when she gently rubbed away the dry blood. He clenched his teeth when she massaged the arm so that the disinfectant could dribble as far into the wound as possible.

Burning pain pulsed through his arm, but he said nothing as she finally dabbed away the last of the blood and put the butterfly bandages in place to hold the holes together in the front and the back.

But when her work was done, and she pulled away, he couldn't let her. He reached for her and pulled her against him.

Her gold-brown eyes went wide with alarm. He couldn't do this. He shouldn't do this. *Forgive me, brother.* He brushed his lips over hers. And as though someone had flicked a switch, he felt no more pain.

Her lips were soft and warm. He was aware of her hands coming up to his chest. More than aware that they weren't pushing him away. Nor did they caress him or pull him closer, but in his current state, her lack of resistance was the only invitation he needed.

He ran his tongue along the seam of her full lips and felt the effect straight to his toes. She'd made him feel as wired, as alive, as acutely aware of all sensations as sitting on that car bomb had. But this was so much more pleasurable.

Her mouth yielded under his pressure and he tasted her at last, feeling as if he had lived his life up to this point for that taste. The thought was too startling and too out of character for him to consider just now. So he simply stopped thinking and, going forward, only felt.

Warm. Silky. Sweet.

His.

Every part of him was clear on that. It wasn't so much a surprise discovery as a quiet recognition. And as he explored her with his tongue, he could lull himself for a while longer into going with the tide and not fighting what every cell in his body was insisting was good and right.

Heat gathered in his groin, heat and need. *Take,* a treacherous voice whispered, then demanded. And he was more than willing to listen to it.

His thumb rested against her pulse as he cradled her face in his hand, and he felt the mad rhythm. His own heart matched it. He kissed her over and over again. Pulled her closer. So close he was no longer sure where his body ended and hers began. And it wasn't close enough.

Honor. The single word popped into his consciousness, which was otherwise filled to the brim with the feel of Julia against him.

Hadn't he just preached about honor not long ago? He had to find his own and in a hurry. He stopped the kiss first, separated his lips from hers with great reluctance, then sucked in air. He let her go then stood abruptly and strode out of the damned storage room.

He had kissed her.

And he had wanted to do more. So much more, wanting it so strongly that it scared him.

He was a man of self-discipline. Surely he had more control than that. For the sake of his brother's memory.

And even beyond that, there were the laws of the

country to consider, common sense and decency. If he let things get out of control, he would be forced to marry her.

And the scary thing was, for a man who had sworn never to wed, the thought didn't seem half-unappealing.

Chapter Six

Her stomach comfortably full with whatever canned food they had shared, Julia pretended to sleep, wondering if she were fooling him at all. Her head was so full of questions, she wouldn't have been surprised if Karim could hear her thinking.

He had kissed her.

What had *that* been about? was the first and foremost question on her mind. How could Karim kiss her like that then ignore her for the rest of the evening? Maybe he always kissed like that. The thought bothered her more than she cared to admit. She didn't want to think about him kissing other women.

Aziz had never kissed her like that. Nobody had ever kissed her like that. She hadn't realized there were kisses that could still make your knees weak hours later in the night.

To say that he surprised her didn't begin to describe how she felt. He'd spent most of their time together up to that point snarling at her and giving her orders. He'd always been cool, and solid, collected. She wouldn't have guessed much could make him lose that iron control, certainly not her.

And she would not have, in a million years, guessed her own response to the man. Something really weird was going on between them. The threat of imminent death, most likely. That was the thing that sharpened all her senses. Subconsciously, they wanted to reaffirm life or something like that. Or it could be that her hormones were the culprit. She'd heard a former co-worker say once that after making her tired and pukey for the first trimester, in the second, her hormones made her incredibly horny.

Julia squeezed her eyes together. Oh, yeah. She was there. Hot and bothered. And nowhere near being able to forget the damn kiss. Give her a year or two. She really hated having no control over her body. And she had a feeling it was going to get worse before it got better.

But no matter what her body wanted, she was *not*, under any circumstances, getting involved with Karim. She was leaving. He just didn't know it yet. And she wasn't interested in getting tangled up in another relationship again. She was going to be a mother soon. She was determined to spend her life trying to be a better mom than her own was, to give all the love and attention to her child she or he needed. From now on, the baby was going to be the focus of everything she did.

She'd tried relationships and failed every single time. She wasn't willing to risk continuing that track record and messing up her baby's life. For as long as this kid needed it, she or he would have her full attention.

But that kiss was— She pushed her lips together when they tingled from the memory. She couldn't afford to think about that kiss.

Definitely not now.

But—

No but.

Maybe—

She sighed into her pillow. Okay. In eighteen years, when the kid went off to college, maybe she would look up Karim.

KARIM WOKE to a scratching noise in the middle of the night, out of a very pleasant dream of kissing Julia again. She'd leveled him without half trying. He couldn't afford to lose his head like that again.

He looked at her across the room on the divan, her hair spread across her pillow. She didn't stir. He slowly rose from his own couch. There were plenty of rooms upstairs, but he didn't want to have her in a separate room from him. Didn't trust her that much. And to share a bedroom with her didn't seem right, although they had already broken so many rules of his country. Having her in the same bedroom with him would have meant the same bed. *Don't think about it.* He didn't trust *himself* that much.

The noise came again.

He pulled his gun from under his pillow, held his breath as he listened, caught a brief shuffle that definitely didn't come from mice. Someone was in the back of the house, near the kitchen.

He stole quietly over to Julia and for a second just

watched how beautiful she looked in the swath of moonlight that illuminated her face. She breathed softly in her sleep. It was the first time he saw her relaxed since they had met.

He needed her awake, and kissing her awake was a sore temptation. But he resisted, putting a hand over her tempting mouth. Her eyes immediately popped open and filled with fear as she struggled against him. But a few seconds later, when she finally recognized him, she stilled. He leaned close to her ear, inhaled her scent of jasmine and vanilla. That scent was going to be the death of him yet.

"Go into the bathroom. Lock the door," he said, then added, "No noise."

He didn't remove his hand until she nodded.

As she crept toward the hall, he stayed where he was and snored softly at first then picked up some volume to cover her movements and the sound of the door when she turned the lock. When he knew she was safe, he eased off on the snoring and moved slowly toward the back of the house.

The moonlight that came in the windows hindered him about as much as it helped. He could see, but it also meant that he would be seen. And the furniture was all pushed around and turned over, all strangeness instead of the familiar shadows he was used to.

He kept to those strange shadows and peered ahead in the semidarkness, hoping to spot the source of the noise. Before he could make any plans, he needed to know how many intruders were in the house. And it wouldn't have hurt to know who they were and with what they were armed.

His left arm was stiff. He rolled it a few times, ignoring the pain. He had to make sure to compensate for the arm. Compensating for his right eye had become second nature over the years, not something he ever needed to think about.

He spotted the intruder as the man slipped from the kitchen, moving toward the stairs that led to the second floor. Young and thin, the guy moved without a sound, his sandals barely touching the floor. There was no other sound. And the guy's body language said he was alone. His gaze darted all over the place, expecting trouble from every direction. He wouldn't have been this jumpy if he had backup.

Karim waited until the guy reached the stairs, climbed and disappeared down the hallway above him. Only then did he sneak toward the kitchen, needing to be one hundred percent sure there was no one else to worry about. He wouldn't leave Julia behind until he confirmed this.

But the kitchen was empty, one of the back windows cut out of the frame, cleverly fooling the security system. It monitored windows being opened, the frame moving away from its place. But with the removal of the glass there had been no need to move the frame at all.

He moved faster now that he knew the intruder was alone, thanking Allah for that favor as he reached the stairs. Gun held in front of him, he took the steps carefully. He could see no one when he reached the top. The long hall had doors to the various rooms on each side, the hallway itself widening into an octagonal sitting room at the end. He had no choice but to check the rooms one by one.

He didn't find the intruder in any of them. *Another floor*. Karim headed toward the stairs again and went up and up, disappointed when he found this floor empty, too.

He nearly turned to rush back to Julia, worried that the intruder had somehow gotten by him and might be a danger to her, when he remembered the attic. His own palace was of traditional Muslim design with its flat roof and the single dome over the middle. But Aziz had some fashionable American designer work on the plans of his home, and the man had added that strange foreign roof line that contained an attic that could be, of course, no use at all in this climate, due to the unbearable heat that gathered up there.

Just past the last room, the attic door was a hidden panel that looked like a piece of carved art, a swirling image of verses from the Quran, decorated with geometric patterns. He found it slightly ajar and eased himself inside.

Heat and stale air hit him in the face, and he thanked Allah that the stairs were made of stone because wood would have dried out long ago and the creaking would have given him away. He made his way to the top.

The large space wasn't empty as he had expected. He stared with surprise at the collection of strange things. The first item he walked by was a stone statue. He couldn't make out much. Barely any light filtered up from the partially open door below. He didn't want to turn on the overhead lamps and give himself away. He couldn't see deep into the attic, but as far as he could see, the place was filled to the brim. It was like a very hot, very dry, overcrowded sauna.

Aziz apparently used his attic to store some of his finds from his amateur archaeological adventures. Odd, really. Karim had been under the impression that everything Aziz had found went into Queen Dara's museum. The country's foreign queen had an obsession for preserving the past—the first thing his countrymen had agreed with her about before she had irrevocably wormed her way into the people's hearts with her many projects.

There were crates up here. Not one of them broken, nor any of the statues disturbed. Whoever had ransacked the house below had not been in here.

But the attic did hold an intruder tonight.

Where was he?

Karim peered into the darkness and tried to breathe in the oppressive heat. He moved forward, passed another statue and realized why these never made it to any museum. Most of the statues depicted human shapes, a practice forbidden by Islam. What on earth was Aziz doing with them?

He heard noise from the back and stole forward, spotted the man's dim flashlight. He stayed hidden behind the crates and statues as he moved forward, careful not to make noise. The attic was enormous, spanning the whole width and length of the palace. A few minutes passed before Karim could make out what the guy was doing. The intruder had a sheet of paper in one hand and the flashlight in the other. He was examining the statues, looking carefully at each one before moving on.

He had both hands full and no weapon that Karim could see.

"Stop," Karim called in Arabic and aimed his gun at the man.

He turned off the flashlight at once, enveloping them in complete darkness. They were too far from the entrance for any light from there to reach them. He heard clothes swish and made a grab that way, but caught nothing but air.

He moved quickly toward the exit, knowing the man would head that way, too, not wanting to become trapped up here. He was about halfway when they bumped into each other at a fair speed. The man went down. Karim saw stars when the guy slammed right into his bullet wound, and lost his own balance, toppling forward as well.

"Who are you?"

He grabbed the man tightly, and they rolled on the floor, bumping into crates. He could have shot the guy, but he didn't want to, not unless he had no other choice. More than anything, he wanted answers.

"Who are you?" he repeated.

The only response he received was a grunt.

They rolled again and something sharp burned his side. A blade? He reached out and found that hand, immobilized it, felt the handle of a knife.

He outweighed the intruder by close to twenty pounds, but the man was wiry. And fought dirty, he realized the next second when the intruder bit his neck hard. Karim brought up his elbow sharply, hit the guy on the chin by chance and heard the man's neck snap back. Then his opponent went limp.

Karim secured the man's hands with his own before he dragged him toward the light, down the stairs.

A youth, barely over twenty. He was shaking off the injury by the time they reached the landing.

"Who sent you?"

The intruder was grubby, most of his front teeth missing, his clothes and hair unkempt. He spit at the floor by Karim's feet and lunged at him. Karim held him back, reached for a curtain pull, yanked it off the wall and tied the guy's hands.

"All right. I'll call the police. They'll know what to do with a thief."

The young man went white. Until recently, the punishment for thievery was cutting off the criminal's right hand in the marketplace. Although most of Beharrain's ancient laws were being reformed, a thief could still count on a severe caning and considerable time in prison.

"In Allah's name I beg you for mercy." The intruder fell at Karim's feet.

"When you tried to kill me, was that in Allah's name, too?" He wasn't impressed by the plea. "Who are you?"

No response.

"Who sent you?" He had a fair idea that he was a street boy turned beggar-slash-thief. How would someone like him know about Aziz's attic? He'd gone straight for it, didn't bother with the rest of the house. How did he know there was something of value up there? And what the hell was it? He hadn't grabbed any of the statues. Looked like he'd been searching for something specific.

"I meant no harm. I was to take nothing." He remained prostrate.

"What were you doing up there?"

"I was given money to find something. That is all. I swear to Allah, that is all." His forehead nearly touched the floor, the back of his shirt stained with sweat.

"Find what?"

"Just some stone. Worth nothing. Just to find them, not to take them. I swear to Allah, sheik."

The man probably had no idea who he was, and was only calling him sheik as a sign of respect. Probably would have done anything to get away. But Karim couldn't let him go.

"Why? Who wants to know what is in Sheik Aziz's attic?"

The man stayed deeply bowed before him.

Karim pulled his cell phone from his pocket, opened it and dialed.

"Abdul Nidal from the *souk,*" the man said quickly, probably fearing the call would go to the police. "Just to look, he said. Just to look." And he paled when Karim didn't shut the phone.

The call was answered on the other end.

"I need you to come to Aziz's palace and pick up someone here," Karim told his chief of security.

The young man looked up, his face now completely white with fear.

Karim dragged him to his feet. He had broken in, had attacked him in the attic, would have killed him if Karim had been slower. All that for a handful of change, most likely. And he would do it again.

His chief of security would figure out who he was and hold him until they knew for sure that he'd spoken the truth. Then they'd see if the police were looking for him for anything. If so, he would be handed over to face justice. If not… Karim would think about giving him a chance and a job at one of the company's oil wells. The men who worked the wells in the middle of the desert were a tough lot. They could handle him.

Abdul Nidal. He turned the name over in his mind. It didn't ring any bells. Then again, there was no reason why it should. He hardly knew every store owner at the *souk,* the local market.

How was Abdul connected to Aziz?

There was only one way to find out.

"NOTHING." Julia kept scanning the floor.

She had followed Karim up after his security picked up the intruder. Four of his men were now stationed downstairs, guarding the house from further disturbance. They were pretty-grim looking men. Hence her preference for the attic, even though the place seriously creeped her out with its eerie statues. Despite the fact that the light was on, the scene still looked like a grave-yard. And it *was* still the middle of the night.

She didn't understand why finding a scrap of paper couldn't wait until morning. Karim was convinced he'd seen some sort of a drawing in the guy's hand when he'd first spotted him, but by the time he caught the man, the intruder had been empty-handed.

Statues and crates loomed in the heat. She tried to stay near Karim, but the whole point was to search different areas of the attic so they could cover ground more quickly. Still, she hated it when he disappeared from sight.

So when had he gone from being a threat—a person she needed to get away from at any cost—to being a point of security for her? Something to think about.

She could not let a single kiss addle her brain this much. But it had been a good kiss. Great. *Beyond great.* She was so busy reliving it that she almost missed the stained piece of paper that had slid half under a crate.

"Found it," she called out, more excited about being able to go back downstairs now than about her find.

Karim was by her side in seconds, taking the crumpled sheet. A careful drawing of four primitively carved statues filled the page, complete with measurements. They were smaller than the ones up in the attic, small enough to be carried by a man, and looked like they might have been made of something different than stone. Their shapes were shaded to indicate color and shine.

Still, they weren't exactly the sort of thing that took your breath away. To her, the larger stone statues of the attic were far more impressive. "What are they?"

Karim shrugged and folded the paper carefully. "I have no idea."

"Can we leave now?" she asked, full of hope. She was exhausted after a tumultuous day. It was about three in the morning. She longed for some more sleep.

Karim watched her for a moment. "You go get some rest. I'll check the crates. I'd rather not involve even my security in this for now. Things like this—" he motioned around "—are controversial in our country's religion. I want to know if Aziz had what our intruder was looking for."

He wasn't the type to quit before he got what he wanted. She'd be smart to keep that in mind.

She drew a deep breath. If he thought she was going back down to his mean-looking guards all by herself, he was nuts. "I guess I'll stay."

He gave her a faint smile, which brought her attention to his masculine lips. And made her wonder what the chances were of repeating that kiss before she somehow broke away from him and made her way home. Probably not very high.

But he didn't walk away from her. "You were scared."

She didn't respond. Of course she was scared. She didn't normally have criminals breaking into places where she was sleeping. And thank God for that.

"I wouldn't have let him get to you." The words were firmly spoken.

She believed him. He was a tougher, harder man than she had ever met before.

And she relaxed fully, finally, realizing only now that the panic of huddling in the downstairs bathroom not knowing where Karim was or what he was doing, not knowing if some assassin was going to kick the door in and shoot her between the eyes the next second, was still there, and that it had settled into her muscles. And when she finally let the fear go, her limbs began to tremble.

She was such a wuss. He was a strong man, probably as disgusted by displays of weakness as her ex-boyfriend, Steve, had been. She tried to still her tremors as she waited for him to walk away.

Instead, he stepped closer and drew her into his arms. "It's okay."

The comfort he gave felt incredibly good. She pressed closer, against the hard muscles of his wide chest, knowing that she should be moving in the opposite direction. Her goal was to get as far away from him as possible. At the moment, she found that goal exceedingly hard to remember.

His hands came to her back to comfort her. Odd that she would feel so incredibly safe in his arms. It had no logic to it. He was not her ally by any means. He meant to keep her prisoner.

She tilted her head to look at him, brought her hands to his chest like she had earlier to push him away. Her hands stayed where they were, like earlier. She couldn't move them all of a sudden. She couldn't move anything. Not when he was dipping his head and she knew that he was going to kiss her again.

This time she braced herself for the effect and it didn't make a damn difference. He still blew her away. The soft brush of his lips against hers aroused her more than anything any other man had ever done to her.

Insane.

Impassioned.

Impossibly good.

A lot of *I*s. There was another one, one that she wasn't going near with a ten-foot pole. *In love*. If there ever was a man who could drag her down that perilous road again, it was the one who could kiss like that. But she did stupid things when she was in love. Handed over her heart and let it get stomped on. If she did another round of that, she was afraid she might not be able to piece it back together again.

No matter how Karim Abdullah made her feel, she could not fall for him. A simple matter of self-preservation. Having had the childhood she had, she was good at self-preservation, wouldn't have survived this long if she weren't.

She *would* leave. But not tonight, she thought and gave herself over to his kiss.

JULIA WOKE TO the sun shining into her eyes through the window, and looked around disoriented. She was lying on a sofa in some sort of an office, Karim working on the computer, intent on the screen.

He looked freshly showered, crisp in a clean suit. The sun glinted off his jet-black hair and outlined his wide shoulders. He radiated power even when he was doing something as mundane as sitting at a desk.

She remembered looking through crates in the middle of the night, and some more phenomenal kissing, the memory of which was enough to set her tingling all over. She must have fallen asleep when she had sat down to rest. And he must have carried her down here.

Her first thought was embarrassment, the second disappointment that she hadn't been awake for it.

"Did you find the statues?" she asked.

He glanced up. "Nothing that looked even remotely similar. But at least I know what they are." A shadow crossed his face.

She sat up and smoothed down her clothes then her hair, although the latter was hopeless.

"They were made before Islam." He pointed to the drawings they'd found in the attic. "My people, the Bedu, had a different religion back then. They worshipped idols. False gods. Today, religious extremists call this time *Jahiliah*—a time of ignorance and evil. They do whatever they can to destroy all history and evidence of these ancient religions."

"That's what the statues are, idols?" she asked. She'd never heard of any of this.

He nodded. "Statues of ancient gods. Back then, when people came to the Kaba stone, they placed their god statues there. When Muhammad came to power, his armies conquered Mecca. He purified Kabba of pagan idols, and the sacred stone became the focus of Islam."

"When you say purified, you mean?"

"Destroyed the idols."

"So to find one is rare?" She was beginning to understand why Aziz's house had been searched so thoroughly, why tonight's intruder had been here.

"Extremely."

"I'm guessing they're worth a lot."

"Their worth is indefinable, but they could be never sold or exhibited in a museum."

"Why?" That made no sense at all. Especially not the museum part. The stuff in the attic was definitely museum material.

"Religious extremists consider them the very devil."

"So those are probably the people who are looking for them, to destroy them."

"Destroy the statues and everyone who has come in contact with them, who had any role in their survival at all. People get rabid about this kind of thing. It probably seems strange to you. But here, for some people, religion is a matter of life and death. Some are willing to die or kill for it."

That took a few moments to digest. She particularly disliked the *kill* part. "How do you know all this?" He hadn't had a clue about the drawings when he'd first looked at that sheet.

"I sent a digital picture to the royal palace."

Oh. Well, the king *was* his cousin.

"Queen Dara identified the statues. What that woman doesn't know about Beharrain's past isn't worth knowing."

How strange, she thought, considering that the queen was born in the U.S. But she was glad that Karim had access to an expert. She wondered if Aziz might have consulted with the queen, as well. Then another, darker thought occurred.

"You think there is a chance whoever is after these statues killed Aziz?" She could still scarcely believe that anyone would want to kill Aziz. Aziz was fun and open and giving. If she had to place bets on who made more enemies between the twin brothers, her money would have been on the Dark Sheik, Karim.

He stood from his desk, his grave expression betraying that he had considered her question already. "I'm becoming more and more sure."

"And now they want you, why?"

"I'm handling my brother's affairs. Since they weren't able to find the statues, they are assuming they've been passed down to me."

He closed his eyes for a moment, his face turning grimmer.

"What is it?"

"You asked after Aziz at the reception at MMPOIL. You were with me in the parking lot, then in the car, then at the hotel. They might think you are involved with this."

"That's insane. I just got here."

"Aziz could have called you to appraise the statues. You could be here to take them to the U.S. Any number of things." He made a gesture of frustration.

"So now they want to get me, too? Just how powerful are these religious extremists?"

His lips flattened into a tight line. "Very."

"And they are coming to get us." Her heart beat in her throat.

"They are not going to stop until they have the statues, and they think we have them."

"But why kill Aziz? Why not capture him and try to get the location of the statues out of him?"

He thought for a second. "They probably thought they knew the location of the statues. They figured if they got Aziz out of the way, the statues would have nobody to protect them."

"But now that they realize they don't know where the statues are, why try to kill you? I mean, if they think you know the location. Wouldn't that be lost if you died? They would never find them."

"They haven't killed me yet," he said darkly. "Not in that chase and not at the hotel. Maybe they were going for capture."

"And the car bomb?" That would have been enough to finish anyone off.

"Remote control," he said pensively. "Wasn't activated until I dove from the car. They wanted to scare me, set me off balance."

"So they want to kidnap you and torture the location of the statues out of you before they kill you?" She felt faint.

His face darkened. "Not just me, I'm afraid. I'm fairly sure that at this stage, they want the both of us."

She thought for a moment. "To be honest, from where I was standing, they didn't look like they were just trying to scare you."

He shrugged. "Maybe not. Maybe they think if they take me out, it'll be easier to get one of my men to talk. I'm sorry that you got involved in this."

She was ready to run for the hills. Her first thought was that he had to let her go now, had to let her leave the country. Her life was in danger here and so was her child's, Aziz's child. She knew he wouldn't be indifferent to that.

But after a moment she realized that if some religious wacko decided to take her out, her simply crossing the border wouldn't stop him. If she'd learned anything from watching the news in the last couple of years, it was that fanatics were more than resourceful and extremely mobile. And even if she left, that would still leave Karim in danger.

She cared only because he was her baby's uncle, she told herself. She had so little family. Really, Karim and the baby were it for now, and the rest of Aziz's family, whom she hadn't met yet. And was in no hurry to do so. If they were anything like Karim, they would want her baby and wouldn't be averse to locking her up and throwing away the key to get what they wanted.

She'd spent years fantasizing what it would be like to have family, people around her that she had a connection to. And now she found some, not a connection of blood, but a connection through her child. Still, a stronger connection than she'd had to anyone in a long time. She'd met only one so far and he was already driving her crazy. And frankly, based upon this initial experience, she was a little scared of meeting the rest of them.

She planned on doing whatever was necessary, in fact, to avoid such meeting and get sucked further into the Abdullah family. Karim was all she could handle. Who was she kidding? The Dark Sheik was more than she could handle. So much more.

And yet she felt obligated to do what she could so the Abdullahs didn't meet a bad end. Family stuff was crazy, she thought, then something occurred to her and she saw a ray of hope at last. Running and hiding would only work for so long. And she didn't want to spend "so long" in this country. She still had her original goal firmly in mind, although her priorities had been reshuffled.

Objective number one: Don't let the crazies capture and kill her.

Objective number two: Get home.

She drew her lungs full of air, wishing she could draw herself full of confidence as easily. They needed a plan. *Think.*

Karim's security could get no more information out of the intruder. They were looking for the man who had supposedly paid him for the break-in. But even that guy might just be another link in the chain and not the one who'd actually put a price on Karim's head.

Okay, here it went. The single idea she'd been able to come up with to get them out of this jam. "What if you found the statues first, and tried to bargain with them?"

Chapter Seven

Karim stared at her. Not a half-bad idea. He liked that she was always thinking—except when she plotted to get away from him—and liked her intelligence. She was the kind of woman any man would be proud to call his wife. Any man who meant to marry. His life was too complicated to allow for that. He funneled his thoughts back to the problem at hand.

If they could locate the statues, they could pretend to bargain with them. He was not willing to hand them over for real. For one, whoever wanted them destroyed would kill him and Julia afterward anyway. Two, he believed in preserving history, whether it was positive or negative, whether he agreed with it or not. Everything had value in life, even one's mistakes. Bad or good, there were always things to be learned from the past.

If he had the statues, maybe he could draw his enemies out into the open with them. Draw them out, identify them, take them out. It was the only way to safety for him, for Julia and her child.

His enemies believed that Aziz had the statues. Having seen the collection in the attic, he was inclined to think that they were right. Obviously, Aziz had found a large pre-Islamic cache he had told no one about.

But someone knew. Aziz's men for one. He hadn't dug out the statues and moved them to the attic on his own. And this Abdul Nidal guy in the *souk*.

He would start with them, Karim decided, and began to plan.

JULIA PACED while Karim made some calls, hating that she didn't understand a word of what he said.

"So?" she asked when he finally put the phone down.

"Abdul Nidal is a disreputable antiquities dealer. His name has been connected to smuggling valuable artifacts out of the country in the past, but there was never enough proof to do anything about it. He is from an old, respected family with connections everywhere. Even the police are reluctant to touch him."

"So there is nothing we can do?" Disappointment tasted bitter on her tongue.

He flashed her an amused look. "I am Sheik Karim."

Then he said something to one of his men, who took off immediately. Next he sent another man away, who returned within ten or fifteen minutes, with boxes of food.

She could have hugged Karim with gratitude as she inhaled the wonderful aromas, saliva gathering in her mouth. Fresh-baked meat, couscous, seasoned rice, fruits and cheeses found their way onto plates.

His men drew back from the upstairs dining room

after setting it right, having picked up overturned chairs and taking out a broken crystal bowl. The two of them were left to eat in private.

Karim seemed preoccupied, but she wasn't sure he'd be in any better mood later, so she pushed ahead.

"I'd like to have my passport back."

"You won't need any identification. While you are here, everywhere you go I'll be with you."

"I'd like to go home. I'm not much use to you in finding the statues. You knew Aziz much better. You'd know better where he hid them. You know the country much better. I would only be in your way."

"You've been through a lot. Rest a few days. We'll talk about this and find a solution."

He didn't mean a word of that, she was sure. He was just playing for time. She hated how unreasonably stubborn he could get. "I have to go back and find another job. I have to pay my rent or they'll kick me out of my apartment and confiscate the furniture." That had been something she'd worried a lot about just a few days ago. Not so much since the threat of imminent death came into the picture. "I have a life back home and the longer I stay, the more thoroughly that will fall apart."

He looked up with an expression that said he hadn't considered that.

"Not everyone lives in their own fully staffed palace." She couldn't help the jab.

"I'll have the apartment taken care of. Just write down the details."

He would? She'd half expected him to say not to

worry about the apartment because she'd be locked up here, a prisoner for the rest of her life. His acknowledging that she would eventually return was a good thing. But he clearly thought it wouldn't happen for a while yet, which was not. "I don't want you to take care of my life."

"If I don't—" impatience made his voice harsh "—you won't have it much longer."

"I'll be safer at home." She wanted to believe that and even succeeded from time to time.

"Will you? Because religious extremists never went to the U.S. to do their dirty business there?"

And she could say nothing to that. The bones in her body seemed to go soft all of a sudden with the thought that he was right, that if these maniacs had set their sights on her, there'd be no hiding from them.

She shored up her defenses against the panic. Those men couldn't want her badly enough to follow her. She had nothing to do with the statues. He was exaggerating. He had to be. He just wanted her scared and compliant so he would get his way.

The words were on her tongue, but she bit them back. If she were to get away from him, it would be better if he thought that she agreed with him, that she'd given up. She went back to her food.

She was just about finished when one of his men came in and said something in Arabic.

"I'll be right back." He stood. "Why don't you stay here and relax for a while."

She didn't respond, only scowled after him, feeling

slightly juvenile. Not that she wanted to be involved in this any more than she already was. As she'd told him, she could be of no use whatsoever. But if he was so sure that her life was on the line, too, he could have at least told her what was going on.

She finished the last of the food on her plate then looked around, took a deep breath. Okay, so Karim had no intention of letting her go. But she had to go, had to go now before the baby was born. Because once her child was born, they would do the test and would know for sure that the baby was Aziz's. Then they would never let her go, or would force her to choose between her freedom and her baby.

An escape now, when she was barely showing, had to be easier than later on when she had twenty or thirty extra pounds on her, or with a baby that she had to hide.

The only tempting thing about staying was the high-quality medical care she would get here. From what she'd seen, sheiks and their families got the red-carpet treatment at the Tihrin hospital. She regretted that she didn't have a job and the health care she could afford from her meager savings was less than stellar. If she didn't succeed in getting work when she got back to the U.S.… She couldn't think about that now. She had to stay positive.

Even if she couldn't get a job right away, everything would be okay. She did have savings. But as a first-time mother, she spent a fair time worrying about what would happen if something went wrong.

She couldn't afford complications.

She pushed her chair back and stood, went to the door to listen. Couldn't hear anything. She opened the door a crack. Nobody seemed to be out in the hallway. She stepped out and crossed over to the end of the railing that looked out over the open space below.

Karim sat on the couch with his back to her. Still, she pulled half behind the wall to her right. She didn't want him to see her if he turned around. Two of his men were standing in front of him. The other two brought a stranger in as she watched.

Karim and his men wore dark suits. The newcomer had traditional robes on and looked decidedly nervous. He bowed to Karim, who offered him a seat, then he said something to his men and they left the room, but somehow the gesture made this seem more threatening than if they had stayed. The visitor must have thought so, too. Julia saw sunlight glint off the beads of sweat on his forehead.

He spoke in rapid Arabic, his eyes shifting to Karim then to the ground, as if he was desperately trying to explain something.

Karim said a single, hard-edged sentence.

Now the man began to protest, his expression wavering between worry and desperation, interspersed with some forced smiles.

Karim asked a question now and then. He didn't raise his voice. He made no threatening gestures. But even so, there was something in his posture, in the way he directed his focus on the man that even made Julia uneasy.

At long last, the man rose from his chair and collapsed at Karim's feet. She couldn't tell from her vantage point if his forehead actually touched Karim's shoes, but it sure looked like it from here.

Then Karim called for his men and stood as they led the visitor away.

He turned, his gaze unerringly finding hers, his face expressionless. Had he known, once again, that she had watched?

Since there was no point in trying to hide now, she stepped away from the wall and walked down the stairs. And realized as Karim walked forward and waited for her—all wide shoulders and intense looks—that medical coverage was not, in fact, the only tempting thing about remaining in Beharrain.

"Who was that?" she asked him as he reached the floor.

"Abdul Nidal. The man who sent that thief in here to look for the statues." He was all business now, all hard angles, focused on whatever plans he was assembling in his head.

"What does he know?"

Karim watched her face for a moment, as if debating whether to tell her or not. Which really galled her, but she kept quiet. Fighting him at every turn would just get his dander up.

"He was contacted by someone who received information that my brother unearthed some valuable items and was asked to locate them."

"Who asked him?"

"The contact was made anonymously, through a carrier."

Her heart sank. She wanted Karim to catch those bastards who'd killed Aziz and very nearly killed her as well. Plus, if he was busy chasing after them, she might have a better chance of getting away. Things would be much easier if both Karim and the bad guys were distracted long enough for her to get out of the country.

Even if she wouldn't be much safer from them at home than here, she would rather face any unpleasantness on her home ground with the full power of U.S. laws and law enforcement to protect her.

"He knew nothing else?" she asked.

"He seemed to think that whoever his customer was, he'd gotten his information from someone close to Aziz. He seemed to have a lot of details about the drawing."

"Do you know who it could have been?"

"Anyone who was there when Aziz made the find. Plus anyone who helped him to move those statues here. He had a regular crew he used when he went out into the desert on one of his treasure hunts." He looked off into the distance. "He was obsessed the last couple of years. First, the king found our great-grandfather's treasures that had been raided from the caravans. Then the king's brother found a whole lost palace." He shook his head. "Aziz was determined that other things were out there, waiting for him. He never lived to see our brother, Tariq, find the last king's hidden hoard of gold bars at his oasis resort in the desert."

"He did have his own find," Julia said.

"That's right." Karim looked up, his face etched with sadness. "I can't believe he didn't tell any of us."

Was that hurt in his voice? Was he close enough to his twin brother that he had expected Aziz to share everything? She had no experience in that department. The last time she had seen her siblings she'd been nine. But losing them still hurt. She couldn't imagine how much it must have hurt to lose a twin after sharing everything for the past thirty years.

"I'm going to start with Aziz's security," Karim said. "They'd been reassigned to the company." And he was dialing already to summon them.

AS IT TURNED OUT, Karim and she returned to Karim's own home under heavy guard where he interrogated members of Aziz's security who'd been ordered to report there. She took a bath and ate another little snack while she waited for him to finish. And when he hadn't come to her quarters to give her an update by noon, she went looking for him on her own, finding him in his office.

He looked up from his computer, his full attention immediately focused on her. "Do you have need of anything? Is everything all right?"

And she blinked for a second, because those weren't questions she'd heard a whole lot in her life. Certainly not from her parents, and not from any of the foster families, either. She had a few trusted friends now, friends who were probably frantic not having heard from her for days. But that circle was a small one. She had trouble taking relationships from businesslike and superficial—which she had mastered with the donors at work—to a more personal level.

Odd that despite being seriously annoyed at Karim, on some level she felt comfortable with him, and that had happened with lightning speed. Perhaps because he did remind her a little of Aziz and because he was her baby's uncle, so in that way they were now related.

After all these years she had family. She couldn't help the grin that split her face.

"Is everything okay?" Karim asked her again, with a look of suspicion this time.

He hadn't seen her smile a lot, or ever, she realized. But, hey, that was his own fault. He shouldn't have kidnapped her.

She had a family member who'd kidnapped her. Someone she was ditching at the first opportunity to escape. Another thought occurred to her. Her newfound family was decidedly dysfunctional. It barely dimmed her smile. Even that sounded so wonderfully real.

"I broke the comb in my room. Sorry." She ran her fingers through her hair to indicate what a tangled mess it was. "Could I have another one? I need industrial strength."

He looked at her for a moment then opened his top drawer and rifled through it. Didn't look as if he found what he was looking for, because he moved on to the next drawer after a few seconds.

"Try this." He held up a shiny object before bringing it over. A pick comb, but not like any she'd seen before. The handle was thick and sturdy, decorated with what looked like turquoise, the whole thing as large as Karim's hand.

She couldn't resist taking it. "It's beautiful. Is it… um…gold?" The piece was obviously handmade, with stunning workmanship.

"I helped the Bedu women of my tribe once with the wool trade. Some of them gave their jewelry, had it melted and remade into this as a thank-you gift."

She tried not to think how much the comb was probably worth, or that it really belonged in a museum. She stuck it into her hair and tried to work the knots out. He probably wouldn't want her to remove the thing from his sight.

He walked back to his desk. "I have the name of the man who most likely betrayed Aziz by selling his secrets. When asked specifically, a couple of security guys remembered that one of the oil well workers who also went on digs with Aziz bragged about coming into money soon, an inheritance from an uncle. They didn't think anything of it at the time. I just checked into it." His attention was on his computer screen again.

"And?" The comb worked amazingly well.

"His uncles are alive and well." His face turned dark.

"So he's likely the one then. Track him down and question him."

"His name was Jusuf. He died at the same well explosion as Aziz."

She sank into a chair while she took that in. A couple of minutes passed before she gathered her thoughts. "Do you think that was on purpose? To get rid of any possible links to the man he worked for?"

Karim leaned back in his chair. "I was sitting here

considering the same thing. Aziz had no business at the well that morning. He could have been asked to go there by his enemies for some made-up reason. He must have gotten suspicious, because he called Tariq and wanted to tell him something but not over the phone. Tariq nearly went out there, but then the chopper broke down."

His face turned darker yet, and Julia remembered that Tariq was his other brother. His only living brother now. If not for the faulty chopper, he could have lost both of his brothers on the same day. The thought of that squeezed her heart, brought back the memory of losing her sisters, suddenly without warning, never to see them again.

"Jusuf, the worker we are suspecting, was reassigned to work at the same well at the last second that morning."

"Do you know who blew up the well?"

"A madman who wanted to take over leading the tribe. A half brother, actually. Long story," he said. "But he is dead now."

The hard glint in his good eye said he might have had something to do with it. Julia chilled from the cold expression on his face.

"Everyone thought Aziz's death was an accident. Collateral damage. But I—"

"Whoever wanted Aziz dead could have known about the well being set up and made sure Aziz and Jusuf were there at the right time," she said.

"That would be my best guess. I already put my men on investigating any possible connections."

She closed her eyes for a minute as she ran all that information through her head. That had to be it. They had to be on the right track. She went back to combing and yanked a strand to make it cooperate.

He stood and walked over, held out his hand. "Let me help."

She only hesitated for a second. When it came to her hair, she could use all the help she could get.

She wasn't prepared for how intimate it would feel as he sank the comb into her unruly mane and worked through the knots one slow stroke at a time. The temperature was definitely rising in the room. Odd that she had never felt like this with her hairdresser. Karim affected her in many unexpected ways.

She needed something to distract herself. Talk.

"So, do many Bedu women have hair like this?" She turned to indicate the sturdy comb, pitying them.

His intense expression softened, and a smile came to hover over his lips as he considered her question. "These kinds of combs are used to comb wool. Not this one. Wooden ones. This was a ceremonial gift."

"Wool, as in sheep?" She made a face.

"Sheep, goat and camel. What's wrong with that?"

"I always knew my hair was bad, but I didn't think I was in the sheep, goat and camel category. It's kind of embarrassing."

He laughed. And she couldn't help staring. It was the first time he had allowed more than a hint of a smile. The sound was warm and deep, resonating in her chest. He stopped too quickly, as if he had surprised even himself.

"Any idea where the statues might be? Could they have

been at the well?" She asked the first question that popped into her mind, to dispel the intimacy of the moment.

"Not likely. We've been rebuilding that. The whole area has been worked over. If anything was there, it would have been found by now."

"Do you know the last place Aziz searched for treasure?"

He made a snortlike sound. "It's not like he had a method. More like he fancied himself the Arabian Indiana Jones. Always searching old scrolls, and taking his findings to Dara and—" He froze midsentence.

"What is it?"

"The week before he died, he was up at the royal palace for dinner. We were supposed to go over some company business that night and I was angry at him for cancelling at the last second. What if—" He was dialing already, and spoke in Arabic first, before he switched to English, his face softening. Clearly he was fond of the person on the other end of the line.

"How are you and the children? I trust all is well with the family." He paused. Listened. "And my cousin?" He listened again.

"Yes. Thank you. Nothing serious. I meant to ask you about that dinner with Aziz before he died. Had he mentioned any new finds?" He paused. "Are you sure?" He shook his head. "Any idea in what area he's been digging?" He listened for the answer. "Thank you…soon…yes."

"So?" she asked impatiently as soon as he hung up.

"Aziz spent some time at our grandfather's cave that

the king and the queen discovered not that long ago."
He didn't seem as excited as she would have expected.
If anything, he seemed troubled. "But that cave had
been completely explored. All the treasure from the
cave, which is in the middle of the desert, had been
removed to the National Museum in the capital city,
Tihrin. And there had never been any statues in there in
the first place. The artifacts gained from there were
much newer."

"Maybe Aziz didn't find the statues there. But
maybe he hid the god statues in that place." She was
thinking out loud.

"Maybe. But it wouldn't make any sense. It's not as
if the cave is hidden anymore. The entrance has been
widened and built out. It's a tourist destination for the
locals. Young people go out on trips to see it. I don't see
any way to hide anything there. But I'll go and check it
in any case. I will leave you protected." He handed the
comb back to her. "You're done. I'll be glad to help
anytime." Banked fire glowed in his gaze.

She felt her temperature rise. She held the comb out,
back to him.

"It's yours." He pushed her hand back gently, linger-
ing for a brief moment with his long fingers on her hand.

"I can't. It's too—"

"It's yours. Now you should rest."

What was it with all the rest, anyway? She'd rested
all morning. She was entering that grace period of pregnancy when the nausea and endless fatigue of the first
trimester had left her, but the bulk and all the aches and

pains of the third trimester were still in the distant future. She felt completely well and energized. She didn't need rest. She needed to go home, something she would see to as soon as Karim left the palace. Except he had her passport. She glanced at his suit jacket.

There didn't seem to be a way to get to that. She had only one other option: going to the American embassy and requesting a new one and their help along with it. Her plane ticket was for a week from now. She didn't want to linger in this country that long. But she was sure they could assist her with that, too.

She felt a brief pang of guilt for deserting Karim in the middle of this mess. But she had nothing to do with it. She had gotten dragged into all this, quite against her will. Her first duty was to her baby. Everything else came second to keeping her baby safe.

"What if whoever is after you is watching your palace?" She didn't want him getting hurt.

"I'll have some delivery made. I'll be leaving in the delivery guy's clothes and car."

Sounded like a plan. "Good luck. I think I *will* rest." She walked to the door. When she turned, Karim's gaze was on her, a speculative look on his face.

She pressed a hand to her abdomen.

The look instantly switched to concern. "I'll have the doctor check on you again. I'll make sure she'll stop in every day while I'm gone."

She took a last long look at him. The thought that she would miss him sounded too crazy to consider. She walked out before she could feel even more guilty about deceiving him and did or said something stupid that would betray her plans.

She hurried down the hallway and didn't slow any when she'd gotten inside her rooms, which were a mess. Karim had a carload of clothes delivered for her, and she hadn't gotten around to picking a personal maid yet and hadn't had a chance to sort everything and find a place for it all to be put away. At this stage, it was something she didn't need to worry about.

She had plenty of other things to occupy her mind, thank you very much.

To get to the embassy, she had to first get out of the palace. Which would be impossible on her own. But Karim was leaving. And his men wouldn't be searching his car. He was going on an expedition, which likely meant he'd be taking lots of equipment if he meant to be digging. The perfect opportunity for one small woman to hide among them. She'd leave at the first red light they stopped for.

She put the comb on the desk in the corner. She couldn't take that, she thought with some regret. Never in her life had she owned something so beautiful. It was too valuable a gift. And it would only remind her of Karim.

She pushed him from her thoughts and braided her hair to keep it out of the way, looked around at her new belongings and chose comfortable slacks and shoes. At the last moment she then grabbed a black, nondescript *abaya*. She should be able to make her way safely to the embassy in that.

She was about to put it on when someone knocked

on her door. She shoved the *abaya* back into the pile.
"Come in."

The door opened to reveal Karim.

"The staff is instructed to take care of you. Anything
you want, you need only to request it," he said.

And she nearly asked if that included her freedom.

Looked like he'd read her intention in her eyes.
"You'll be safe inside the gates."

She shrugged. Let him believe that she'd given up.

He moved closer, stopped a few inches from her, his
gaze burning into hers. The air grew thick between
them, got stuck in her lungs. His good eye searched her
face. She could smell the scent of his sandalwood soap,
could feel the heat of his body. He was close, too close,
too intense, too easily reading her mind.

"Don't."

"Don't what?" She played the innocent.

"I don't want you to get hurt. Don't try to leave
while I'm gone."

"I won't." And she wasn't lying. She would be
leaving *with* him.

He shifted, as if ready to walk away, but stayed where
he was, holding her gaze.

Heat gathered between them. His gaze dropped to her
lips. The heat dropped to the V of her thighs.

She desperately wanted him to kiss her, knowing it
would be the last time. She would be gone by the time he
returned from his trip to the desert. She swayed forward
a little. He stayed where he was. How disappointing.

"This thing—" he started to say.

"It's not a good idea," she finished.

Not that either of them moved back an inch.

"I don't seem to be able to help myself," he admitted as he lowered his head at last.

She knew how he felt.

But in the next second, she forgot all she knew, the only thing real being the feel of his lips against hers. He was gentle, incredibly gentle as he always had been. But soon a fiercer undertone crept between them, and the heat increased, and he didn't cajole anymore. He took.

She could feel the whole of his need in that kiss, and it shook her, because it said he wanted to take more, wanted to take it all. And in that moment, she was willing to give it, mindlessly losing herself to him.

Then the kiss changed again, to that of possession and branding. He was claiming her. She didn't have it in her to protest.

She was struggling to find any control at all by the time he finished with her, hell, struggling just to stay upright. But before she could even catch her breath, he was leaning low again, and she braced herself for the next assault on her senses.

But when his lips reached dangerously close, instead of claiming her again, they parted to issue a warning.

"There is no place you could run where I wouldn't find you."

Chapter Eight

The plan had been great and it could have worked. The delivery truck had canvas flaps for sides, easy to get in and out of. And since the truck bed sat low to the ground, it wouldn't have been difficult to jump off once the vehicle stopped at a red light. Julia had gotten into the very last crate, a large one right next to the tailgate. It held ropes and a pickax. The only mistake she'd made was not realizing how much equipment Karim meant to take. At the last minute, he'd put a box on her crate. Then a box on top of that. Enough weight so she couldn't push it aside.

Luckily, her crate had plenty of cracks in it so she could breathe. But the pickax dug into her side. Her limbs were going numb. They'd been traveling for hours, and she was thirsty and hungry. She could have brought food and water—there'd been plenty of it in her room—but as she had planned on parting company with Karim within minutes of him driving through the palace gate, she hadn't. She had to go to the bathroom so badly her eyes were crossing.

The space was too uncomfortable to sleep, too small to move. She hadn't cared back when she'd gotten in, just considered herself lucky that there was enough room for her. She hadn't known that she would be spending hours in there. Now she cursed her rash decision.

She'd been rash because she'd been desperate. She'd been desperate because of Karim. The way his kisses made her feel notwithstanding, he'd been nothing but trouble since she'd set eyes on the man. And how dare he kiss her, anyway? She had plenty of time and felt plenty miserable to have worked herself up to a good, righteous anger. To hell with Karim, she thought just as the car stopped.

Kind of lurched to a stop, actually, rattling her in the crate. Had they arrived or was something wrong? Desert bandits came to mind. The receptionist at the Hilton had warned her about them, after giving her some flyers at check-in that listed all the fun activities one could do in Tihrin, including guided desert tours. Apparently, there'd been recent attacks. Which hadn't bothered her much at the time, as she hadn't intended to do any sight-seeing, especially not in the desert. Her plan had been simple: get in, see Aziz, get out.

The door on the truck's cab slammed shut.

She listened for voices as she grabbed for the handle of the pickax.

"WHAT ARE YOU doing here?" Karim growled as Julia awkwardly climbed out of one of the crates with a pickax in her hand.

She moved slowly. Her legs had probably fallen asleep. She looked a little peaked all around, her full lips parched. "Fighting for my freedom," she said, looking very much like a woman on the edge.

Did hormones do that? Make pregnant women utterly unreasonable? He hoped so. Didn't want to think that she would be like this *all* the time. She could be the mother of his nephew, after all. But, by Allah, she was a lot of trouble, more perhaps than she was worth. And for a moment, he couldn't understand what Aziz could have possibly seen in her.

Then she raised the pickax and her eyes flashed their golden-brown depths, her amazing hair having come undone from its braid, flitting in the breeze. And he had to admit that even as unreasonable and disobedient as she was, she was magnificent.

"Relax." He took the ax from her.

"When we stopped, I thought maybe the bad guys caught up with us. Or you ran into bandits."

So the ax hadn't been for him. Good to know.

"I saw tracks in the sand. This is the last place where Aziz had been digging. We're in the middle of the desert. People come out now and then to see the cave, but not that often. The tracks could be meaningful, maybe. I didn't want to run them over. I want to look at them and see if I can figure out anything." Now, however, he was considering turning around and taking her back home before he did any investigating out here at the cave at all.

Except, she looked as if she could use a break. The

long drive back was more than she should be subjected to right away. He swore under his breath then carefully swooped her into his arms and carried her into the cave, into shade, keeping his eyes on the tracks that looked a few days old on closer inspection. Two cars, a handful of men. No sign of anything having been dragged out of the cave.

She wouldn't put her arms around his neck, but she leaned against his chest to balance her weight. She felt light in his arms, too light, making him wonder once again if she was eating enough.

"How are you feeling?"

She lifted her head and flashed him a scathing look. Apparently, she felt good enough to fight him every step of the way. She thought she fought for her freedom. He bit back an annoyed remark. Then paused. If their situations were reversed... A crazy thought. He was a man, a sheik. He did not need anyone's protection, while she was obviously in desperate need of it.

He could have put her down as soon as they were in the cave, but he walked to the back with her, not wanting to let go. She felt fragile pressed up against him, bringing out protective instincts. Her full breasts were plastered against his chest, bringing out another response altogether. He wanted to kiss her again, wanted more, but the scowl on her beautiful face warned him that this might not be the best time.

He placed her gently on a large, flat rock. "I'll bring you some food and water."

She was looking around with a disappointed frown. "This is Aziz's cave?"

"The antechamber, so to speak." He brought a bottle of water from the cooler his cook had packed, and handed it to her.

She drank deeply, then looked around again. "Where is your security? I thought you would bring at least two guys. Two could have fit in the truck's cab."

"One man came in the delivery truck, so the least suspicious thing to do was to have one man leave in it. If I jammed the cab with security personnel, whoever is watching the palace would have known something was not right. And I wanted to leave as many men behind to protect you as I possibly could," he said with some exasperation.

His response seemed to give her pause, but she recovered pretty quickly. "Are you sure your enemies won't figure out that you left the palace if they don't see you move around for a while?"

"I put the word out that I'm recovering from a gunshot wound."

She fidgeted. Bit her lip. Shuffled her feet on the ground. "I have to go to the bathroom."

"You can go behind the rock that tops off the cave." He had driven around it to make sure the area was empty on all sides. They were alone. "Don't spend too much time out in the sun," he added, then turned from her and walked outside to unload the truck.

She seemed to be all right. They were already here. A preliminary search through the lower chamber of the cave shouldn't take more than an hour or two. At least he would know what he faced when he came back later. He might need more tools. It only made sense that he looked around while she rested. Time was not to be wasted. The sooner he got to the end of the mystery of the idols, the sooner she would truly be safe.

He brought in the crate she'd been hiding in, moving awkwardly due it its sheer size, appreciating that the temperature was twenty degrees cooler inside the cave. He glanced around the cavern, which had been expanded to accommodate visitors. He'd never found this part of the cave particularly impressive. He was on the third crate when she joined him, carrying a canvas bag.

"I don't want you to lift anything heavy."

She rolled her eyes. "It's bread and dried food."

He took the bag from her nevertheless.

She walked away from him, looking at the sheer stone walls, the path to the corner and the hole that led to an underground chamber of the cave, a sole rope dangling there for support.

"I'm guessing that's where we are going."

Did the thought scare her? Good. "You should have seen the place before it was remodeled. King Saeed, who discovered the cave, said the way down was a rabbit hole carved in the rock. You squeezed through dark passages that led to small enclosures barely large enough to sit up in. There you had to find the opening of the next tunnel, excavate it and move forward."

She looked suitably impressed.

"Anyway, I'm going down there. You're staying up

here." He headed out for the last crate that held equipment he figured he would need even for a quick look around.

"And if somebody comes?" She stared down the hole, into the darkness, her shoulders tense.

He slowed and considered. Somebody *could* stop by. Even if they weren't the people who wanted them dead, there could come a party of young men, the kind who sometimes drove deep into the desert for drunken parties their fathers wouldn't allow at home since alcohol was illegal in Beharrain, as in most Muslim countries. She would be up here alone—

He had made plans for her. Left her under guard. Safe. Of all the insane things she could have done— Frustration made him stop what he was doing and turn around. "Why are you here?"

"You have my passport," she said evenly, as if she were being completely reasonable.

Stubborn. She was exceedingly stubborn, that was what she was. He had made a mistake by not taking that into consideration, by assuming that she would heed his words at least to a degree, because she was a woman and his sole intention was to protect her, and not the least because he was a sheik and everybody else heeded his words. Damn.

"I'm a little scared staying up here alone." She looked away.

And he could tell that it cost her to admit that.

"Don't worry about it. I'll stay right here until you rest, then I'll take you back home. I can come back here later."

"Tomorrow?"

He nodded. By the time he got back to his palace, the day would be pretty much over.

"It would cost you the whole day," she said, sounding dismayed.

He shrugged. It couldn't be helped.

She looked down into the darkness again. "I could go down there with you. I'm not completely helpless, you know."

Far from it. She'd outsmarted him and had gotten out of his closely guarded palace without anyone catching her. "I don't think it's advisable in your condition."

"I don't have a condition." She scowled. "I'm not sick. I'm pregnant." She had stubborn written all over her face.

"Can you climb rope?" He indicated the hole against his better judgment. In truth, if she got tired, he could carry her down on his back. She weighed nothing.

"Can you act insufferably imperious?" She drew herself straight in response to his challenge.

She was funny.

He was not.

He'd had few light moments in his life, was aware that he'd grown up to be a harsh man, hadn't questioned it much. Until now.

Aziz had liked to joke. Strange how the same childhood experiences could form two very different men. Aziz sought to make up for his bleak past with jamming as much adventure and excitement as possible into his life. Karim couldn't forget. He coped with the past by being involved in the law-making process in what little time his corporate job at MMPOIL left him. As sheik, he had input into the judicial reforms, and he took advantage of that to make sure that what his stepbrother had done to his family and his country, could never happen again. His only entertainment was the occasional trip to the camel races.

He wondered what Julia would think of that. She'd find his life unbearably boring, no doubt. She was stubborn and feisty, but by Allah, with all that wild hair and that determination in her eyes, she was a sight to behold. He couldn't help the smile that tugged up the corner of his lips. And she smiled back in response and visibly relaxed, and something passed between them, a moment, a sort of understanding.

He realized that until now he'd been too angry at her for stowing away to see that she'd been scared. Of the desert? Of him? She'd be smart to be cautious on both counts. But she had no cause to be scared of him. Allah only knew what nonsense her head had been filled with, growing up in the West.

"All I wish for is your safety." Maybe if he said it enough times, it would reach her at some point.

She gave no indication that she believed him, but at least she didn't fight his declaration, either. "Let's go," she said.

"I'll go first." He lifted a sack that had been filled to the brim with essentials and clipped it to his belt. "It's about fifty feet down. If you need to stop and rest at any time, let me know."

He found the hole in the rock for the safety line and put in a pin and attached a second rope. Then he sat on the edge of the hole and grabbed the original rope that was fastened to a steel stud someone else had driven into the rock. He shifted his weight onto the rope carefully. It was a sturdy piece and held. When he was a couple of feet down, he turned his flashlight on and let it hang down his belt, pointing to the cave floor below, then called up to her to follow.

He watched as she came over, moving gracefully, and caught up with him in no time.

"Everything okay?"

"Perfectly fine," she said.

When they got halfway down and she hadn't called for rest yet, he stopped on his own. "You can put your feet on my shoulders and take your weight off your arms."

"I don't have to. I'm okay."

"Humor me."

"You already have that bag hanging on you."

"I can handle it."

"So why can't you believe that I can handle it?"

Stubborn. He could be that, too. "The sooner you take a break, the sooner we can move on."

She murmured something he couldn't catch, but she did move down, and her slim feet came to rest on his shoulders for a few seconds.

"Okay. I'm good now," she said too soon.

He made her rest another minute before he continued downward.

The underground cavern they landed in was ten times larger than the one above. The sounds of running water came from the back, and a small pool came to view as they moved forward on the uneven floor. This was the attraction that drew visitors.

"Wow." She was staring wide-eyed at the area his flashlight illuminated.

He'd had the same reaction the one time he had come down here. It seemed amazing that all this should be hidden under the arid desert above.

"According to Queen Dara, Aziz spent a whole week here not long before his death." He panned the area with his flashlight.

"What did he do?"

Exactly. What did Aziz do in a bare cave for a week? Aziz had never been the introspective, meditative type. He lived for excitement. What excitement could he have possibly found here that held his attention for a full seven days?

Karim had a fair idea. "I think he might have found another passage. When Saeed came across our grand-father's hidden treasure down here, it was such a surprise that nobody looked much beyond it. What they carted off to the National Museum was staggering. It wouldn't have occurred to anyone to look for more."

"Why would it occur to Aziz then?" She cocked her head.

Good question. "He was always studying ancient scrolls. Could be he found some information in those." No way to tell. He'd spent a couple of hours looking for some of his scrolls while he and Julia had stayed at Aziz's palace, but had found nothing. Whoever had ransacked the palace had taken those, along with who knew what else.

"So we look for another passage." Julia was already walking toward the rock wall.

"You can check around the perimeter and see if you find something. If you do, do not go anywhere. Watch out for large crevices in the cave floor so you don't fall in. Here." He tossed her the flashlight and she caught it.

"And you?"

"I'll get the rest of our equipment down here."

KARIM'S INITIAL estimate of one to two hours for a quick scan turned out to be optimistic. The cavern was larger than he had remembered. They searched late into the evening, with him persevering in getting Julia to take regular breaks, since she refused to leave until they examined every inch of the cave wall. He'd even set up ropes to check higher up all around. They'd found nothing.

"This is it." He rappelled back down to her. "I don't know where else it could be."

She was standing at the water's edge. "Mind if I take a dip before we go back? The ride will take hours yet. I can't believe how hot and sweaty I am."

The images that flickered through his mind froze his hands to the harness for a second.

"Trust me, you would not want to sit close to me for the next couple of hours."

Just because she was an intelligent woman, didn't mean she couldn't be at times utterly wrong. He would have liked to be as close to her as possible. Closer.

"Go ahead." He carried the harness to the area of the

cave where a wall of boulders blocked the pool from view, and considered the trip back to occupy his mind. A couple of hours in the car. And she looked exhausted already. He'd been telling her to rest, but here he was, planning to drag her all over creation for hours yet.

He made up his mind and went to the crate he had lowered earlier because it contained most of his pulleys. As luck would have it, he had wrapped his equipment in his sleeping bag along with a couple of blankets. He had planned to spend a night or two here before he'd known that she would be joining him. They could stay a single night, he supposed, and start on their return journey in the morning, refreshed.

He was blocking thoughts of Julia naked in the water so vehemently, that he hadn't heard her come up behind him and was startled when she asked, "Do you have a towel I could use?"

She hadn't even undressed yet.

He could get her there. In seconds. About three would be enough. Instead, he drew a slow breath, removed a towel from the crate and handed it to her. "Here."

"Thanks."

He shouldn't have turned to watch her walk away, but he found himself leaning against the crate. She took his flashlight with her, the swinging light outlining her sil-houette. She wore her slacks and tunic, her shapeless *abaya* discarded at the top of the cave. She wouldn't have been able to climb the rope in that.

He couldn't look away until she disappeared behind the boulders. Then he pulled over one of the dozen cave lights he had strategically placed on the floor, and began to set up the few supplies he had. Since he'd planned on spending only a couple of nights—alone—he had brought little.

He was done and sitting on their bedding by the time he heard water splashing at the back of the cave. He clenched his jaw, his hands going still on the food bag. He drew a deep breath, looked up in the direction of the ceiling he couldn't see. The lights he had weren't powerful enough to light the whole cavern all at once. They'd been working in sections. "Take your time. We'll stay the night. You need your rest. It's too hot out there for another long ride," he called out to her.

She didn't respond. Probably didn't like being told what to do, yet again. He couldn't afford to worry about that. His first priority was to protect her and her child.

He closed his eyes and tried to picture Aziz in this cave, what he had found and how he had found it. Images of Julia Gardner naked in the water kept breaking in. She was beautiful, strong, honorable, smart. He wanted her, there was no denying that. He wanted her and was jealous of Aziz that he had found her, that she had fallen in love with him, that she was carrying his child.

"Karim?" Her voice reached him from a distance.

He opened his eyes, and for an insane moment held his breath that she might ask him to join her in the pool. The hope of it alone was enough to make his body harden. "Yes?"

"I think I found something."

SHE WAS OUT OF the water by the time he reached her, and partially dressed. Her tunic came to midthigh. She hadn't put on her slacks yet. He tried not to stare at her shapely limbs and failed.

"What is it?" He dragged his gaze upward at last.

"Look." She squatted and pointed at the rock with her flashlight where a hole had been drilled about the width of a finger.

He squatted next to her to examine it, looked around and soon found another.

"Do you think it's marking something? What do you think it means?" she asked.

He knew exactly what it meant. His mind was moving a mile a minute. "There was a hook for a rope here, and a backup rope." He peered into the water then stood to shed his shirt, shoes and socks, leaving only his pants. He slipped in.

"There's an undertow there," she warned when he had resurfaced. "That's why I grabbed on to the edge and my finger slid into the hole."

He stood right in the undertow and felt the wall of the pool with his hand. Solid rock. Then he extended his right foot forward and felt a crevice. He dipped under, and found a tunnel that started on the pool's floor and was about three feet wide and tall. He couldn't get to the end of it, the flow of water working against him, carrying him out. He gave up after another moment and broke the surface for air.

"I think I found an underwater passage. That's how this pool is fed. The water is coming from there."

"Did you bring scuba equipment?" She glanced up. He still had crates on the truck he hadn't removed.

"Everything but."

"You can come back another time."

He wasn't going to turn around without giving this a serious try. He pulled himself out of the pool and brought over two ropes plus a helmet with a waterproof light attached to it. He fastened that on first, then set the ropes up and secured himself before slipping back into the water. "Hang on to this." He handed her the end of one of the ropes. "One tug, I'm okay. Two tugs, pull me back."

"I don't think—"

"This could lead someplace."

"Maybe Aziz had proper gear."

"But the people who hid those statues hundreds of years ago didn't. If they could get through so can I."

"Hundreds of years ago, the cave could have been dry. Don't things in the earth shift over time?"

She was right. But still, he had to try. "I'll come back." And with that, he took a deep breath and went under.

He could see much better with the light on. The tunnel was slightly smaller than he'd previously judged, but as far as he could tell, he wouldn't have to worry about getting stuck. He kicked away with all his strength, swam against the current, pushing against the tunnel wall with his feet.

He pushed again, got jerked back and realized his rope had gotten caught on something. He had to turn around to free it, losing a few feet as the current pushed him back. Using all his strength, he kicked away.

Nothing but water and rock for as far as he could see.

Had Aziz been here? Were those screw marks by the pool his? Other possible explanations came to mind now. Maybe after they'd emptied the cave of treasures, the archaeologists had dredged the pool. He hadn't followed the proceedings closely, knew most of what he did from the media.

He wondered if he'd been in a full minute yet. Time had stopped as soon as he'd entered the tunnel. It seemed he'd been here long, too long already. But that couldn't be. It didn't seem he'd gotten all that far. He pushed forward again.

Rock and water. *Push.*

His lungs began to burn. He spotted some sort of obstruction ahead. He would just go that far and see if that was the end of the tunnel, if it narrowed down so much that passage was impossible. That way, they would at least know this was a dead end.

He held his breath and moved forward until jagged rocks protruding from the bottom blocked his way. Only one way to figure out if he could get through. He pushed through them carefully. The space was impossibly small now, his air all but gone. He shoved his body forward. He would give this a good try then yank on the rope and between the water pushing him out and Julia pulling, he should be back in the pool in no time.

Unless Julia had taken her passport from his wallet, climbed up the rope and was even now driving the van away from here. He shut the uneasy thought down.

Some of the rocks were loose, he realized, and tried to

roll one out of the way with little success. Had Aziz blasted in this section so that nobody could come back here?

He twisted and his rope got caught again. No, not the rope, he realized after a moment as protruding rocks scraped his side. He'd gone too far.

And now he was stuck.

Chapter Nine

Without having a watch, it was hard to tell how long he'd been underwater, but it sure seemed like a long time. Julia glanced toward her sandals at the other end of the pool, her wristwatch on top of them. She considered running over there and grabbing it, but she didn't dare let go of the rope in case Karim signaled that he needed her help.

Her best guess was that more than two minutes had passed since he'd submerged. Had to be more than that. She tugged on the rope tentatively. It gave. Too easily. And she knew without a doubt that there was nothing on the other end.

Maybe the rope had gotten tangled and Karim had to cut himself free. She tried the security rope. That one didn't give at all, stuck. She yanked as hard as she could. All she got were rope burns on her palm.

"Karim!" she called, knowing he couldn't hear her, getting panicky now. "Karim!" She yanked frantically at the rope.

He was overbearing and bossy and very difficult to deal with. There'd been a time when she would have been happy to be rid of him, but now she wanted him back. His stubbornness aside, he was a good man, he really was. He was honorable, he cared for others, he stood on the right side.

Dozens of images flashed through her mind. Some had to do with the way he had protected her from the assassins, others with the way he had kissed her. She let go of the rope and slipped into the water as she was, not wanting to waste time taking off her clothes. "Hang in there," she said to the water.

She couldn't give up without trying to get him out.

THE FIRST THING he heard over the ringing in his ears when he broke surface was Julia yelling, "Where have you been?"

The first thing he registered was relief that she was still there. He grabbed on to the side of the pool and gulped air, trying to catch his breath.

"What happened to your ropes?" She was in the water with her clothes on.

Had she jumped in to pull him back?

"Had to cut one when it got tangled." He helped her out then dragged himself up on the rock next to her, still breathing hard. "The other one I tied out as a lead line."

She stared at him, her face awash in the remnants of fear then relief. She cared whether he lived or died. That came as a surprise. He would have thought the only thing she cared about was getting away from him.

She had tried to save him. The wet clothes plastered to her tempting body were a testimony to that. And it hit him suddenly what could have happened to her, venturing into that passage without a rope, without anyone watching out for her.

If he had gotten out of the water on the other side, if he had tarried instead of coming straight back... She could have gotten stuck. She could have...

He stood to shake off the gut-wrenching feeling that came from that thought. And when she stood, too, still visibly shaken, he couldn't help taking her into his arms.

He could feel the rapid beating of her heart against his chest, and he held her until it slowed, a moment passing between them, an understanding of what they could have lost. He *hated* the thought that he could have lost her just now. How easily he could have lost her a number of times since she had walked into his life.

"Lead line to where?" she asked after a while as she pulled away, curiosity having replaced fear in her eyes. Trust her not to overlook a thing.

The tension in his shoulders eased and he grinned. Because what he had found was so unbelievable he couldn't help himself. "Another cavern."

"Are the idols there?"

And now that the tension of what could have happened leaked out of the moment, he registered nipples protruding under her wet top, and got momentarily distracted. Of course, the helmet light was still on, spotlighting whatever he turned his head toward. He reached up and turned it off. "The place is too big. I need more lamps."

"I'm coming, too."

Again, hard to focus with those perfect breasts not two feet from him. Deep breath. "No."

"You might need help."

He needed a lot of things right now. None of which she would willingly give, he was betting. "I won't."

"You lost your rope."

"I had backup."

He considered telling her to take her clothes off before she caught a cold. But the air in the cave was a comfortable temperature. And truth be told, Julia Gardner without clothes was more than he could handle.

She was glaring at him, pursing eminently kissable lips. "My baby's father died for whatever is in that cavern. I'm coming."

He drew another long breath, sobered by her mention of Aziz. "Were you in love with my brother?" Suddenly, it was important to know.

"No. I—" She closed her eyes for a second.

He nodded, feeling immeasurably lighter, then feeling guilty about it. "I won't be long." With some luck.

"I can come after you anyway. You can't keep me here." She flashed him a *so there* look.

Technically, he could. He could tie her up, worst came to worst. But he didn't want to. Truth was, he had an idea that something extraordinary waited on the other side of the passage. And he wanted to share that with her.

He didn't dare closely examine that piece of insanity.

"Fine." He would have liked to argue further that it wasn't safe, that she should be careful in her condition.

But her condition hadn't slowed her down so far and, Allah knew, just mentioning that word to her was dangerous enough. The tunnel wasn't too bad now that he had cleared the obstruction. They should be able to get over to the other end relatively fast with the help of the lead line he'd left.

His gaze dipped to her breasts again. Damn, that was it. He looked up with effort. "Get packing," he said.

"THERE ARE VISITORS at the cave."

Mustafa paged through a religious newspaper as one of his men reported over the phone. He had his followers patrol all of Aziz Abdullah's latest digs. They had searched them thoroughly, finding nothing. But he hadn't given up yet. He had a strong, holy purpose and it gave him strength to see the task through, no matter how difficult it was becoming nor how long his mission stretched out.

"Who is it?"

"I don't know. I can only see the truck. Should I go in?"

"No." Mustafa dropped the paper and rubbed his burning eyes. "What kind of truck?"

"Delivery. White and yellow."

His fingers tightened on the phone. The only vehicle that had left Karim Abdullah's palace in the past twenty-four hours had been a white-and-yellow delivery truck.

"It's him." His pulse quickened at the knowledge of how close he was to his prey now. Karim was out in the middle of the desert. Possibly alone. Only a single driver had been reported leaving with the truck, although he couldn't be sure that some of his men hadn't hidden in the back. Still, the number of guards he could have taken was limited.

"I could go in and find him," his man offered.

"Wait outside. Report if anything changes. I'll be there as fast as I can."

He couldn't trust his man to take care of Karim. Karim was a true warrior, a worthy adversary. Mustafa stood. He would bring backup. And he couldn't trust his man with the idols, if they were in there with Karim. Those idols had corrupted two eminent sheiks already. Who knew what power they had over lesser men?

Only he should be the one to handle them. Allah had chosen him for that glorious task.

JULIA'S CHIN was hitting her chest as Karim lit the last lamp and the full magnificence of the new cavern was finally revealed. The water that fed the pond she'd bathed in did, indeed, come from here. An underground stream broke the rock high above her, creating a stunning waterfall before collecting into the larger pool at her feet that was connected to the pool in the cavern they'd come from.

Next to the fall, black rock rose up as far as they could see, its dark color a contrast to the rest of the cave. As Karim directed a lamp at it, the stone sparkled.

"Some kind of granite," he said.

But her attention was focused on the niches carved out of the granite, four perfect indentations, six inches wide and about a foot tall, overlooking the pool. Each niche held a carved and painted figure she couldn't quite make out from the distance. They were situated so they would be at the focus of attention, everything leading toward them, even the odd undulations of the rocks, the cracks in the ground and on the cave wall.

But as Karim raised the light and panned it, she realized that those cracks and other shadows were not random, nor were they natural. Man-made patterns decorated nearly every square foot of the cavern. And as she looked down at her feet, she realized that the lines she stood on, too, were part of some bigger whole. As she walked forward, following it with the lamp on her helmet, she realized she was moving through a garden.

Pictures depicting plants of all shapes and sizes covered the floor, some with familiar leaf motifs, others she'd never seen. Animals hid in the grass and behind bushes. Trees towered on the side with exotic birds sitting among the braches. All of that faced the four niches. And all, from the smallest parrot to the largest tree, seemed to have this awed feel to it, as if they were in the process of worshipping.

The closer she got to the granite, the thicker the air felt, heavier. She stopped, feeling like an intruder at an ancient, secret ceremony. She felt a distinct sense of being pushed back and down, to the ground. "What is this place?" She couldn't raise her voice above a whisper.

Karim stood completely still, in that warrior readiness state of his she'd seen before. "A pagan temple."

She could believe it.

"And that?" She motioned toward the granite rock

with the four carved images that appeared to have
some human features. They looked similar at first
glance, but upon closer inspection, she could tell that
two were definitely male and two female. They had
large, round eyes painted in white that took up most
of their faces.

"I'm guessing those would be the idols. See that?"
He pointed up to a circular hole in the wall above the
four figures, at an empty niche she hadn't noticed before
as it was well above eye level.

"What do you think was there?" The drawing from
the thief who'd broken into Aziz's palace only depicted
the four idols.

"I don't know, but look." He went to the back of the
cave.

She moved over to him.

"The patterns seem to come in stripes." He pointed
to the ground and the cave walls. "Connected to the
niches like sun rays." He walked forward several feet.

She examined each picture they walked over, and the
farther they went, the more she understood what he
meant. There were definitely several themes here. The
first section was the darkest and scariest. She hadn't
come back this far before and now noticed that the
"forest" she had stood in had disappeared. The shadows
were deeper, the rocks more jagged. The drawings re-
sembled weapons and twisted limbs and torsos, faces
distorted in pain, bones, in places piles of them.

She moved closer to Karim and stuck to him. "What
do you think it means? Could be a warning to anyone

who violates this place." Kind of like Indiana Jones and the Temple of Doom, she thought and shivered when she remembered that the last person who'd been here before them, Aziz, was now dead.

"I don't think so." Karim turned toward the darkly glittering granite. "It's all connected to that first niche, to that god statue that's in there. I'm guessing he might have been the god of war or something like that."

Could be. She moved out of the "war zone" as quickly as possible.

The next swatch of images seemed like an ancient city, a jumble of mud brick dwellings. She felt easier treading among those, until she noticed a large dark circle to her right. Karim caught her gasp and moved that way immediately.

"Charred rock. Something has been burned here."

"You think Aziz—"

"My brother might have been only an amateur archaeologist, but he would have known not to violate a find. He would not have camped here and lit a bonfire." He squatted and ran his finger over the dust and ashes. "This is much older. Not just the ashes of one fire but many."

They moved on to the next section, but the geometrical patterns of this she could not begin to recognize. She looked at Karim. He simply shrugged.

The last section, belonging to a goddess, encompassed the waterfall and the pool, leaving little room for drawings. But, although the available surface was much smaller, the ancient artist or artists had been determined to overcome that handicap; not a rock was left un-adorned here. This was the magical forest she'd seen when she'd first looked around. The picture was teem-ing with life.

"The Garden of Eden?" she asked.

"You could say that." He moved forward. "I'm guessing this quadrant belonged to some goddess of fertility."

That explained the appearance of human forms as they neared the pool, always in pairs, always touching.

He stopped at the edge of the water. "This could be where they performed fertility rituals."

And the way he looked at her suddenly sucked the air out of her lungs. Thinking about Karim and fer-tility rituals at the same time, and looking at the suggestive images all around them, was scrambling her brain big-time.

"Um. Okay." She stepped back too quickly and almost slid into the water.

Karim steadied her elbow. And kept his hand there.

"So I guess we can go back then." She slipped away from him, hoping that if she moved beyond his reach, maybe her brain cells would return to work.

"I think we should sleep here." He watched her.

"Here?" Her voice positively squeaked.

He pointed at the pool. "Water." Then toward the area where the charred circle was. "Fire."

"Earth. Air," she finished for him. "The four elements."

His first response was a smile. "Feel that?"

"What?"

"The air. There is fresh air here. A flow of air. Which means there might be a small opening to the outside. It's dark out there right now, so we can't see anything. Tomorrow morning when the sun comes up, we could see where the air comes from."

"And?"

"If air can come in, maybe sunshine can, too. Maybe it will illuminate some portion of these drawings that will give us a clue to the round item that is missing. I want to be here at first light. I want to see where sunshine falls when the sun is highest in the sky. I'd like to see what the last rays illuminate in the evening."

"We can't sleep here," she protested weakly.

"I have some waterproof bags. I'll bring our sleeping bags and some food over. You pick a spot."

She so didn't want to. But she looked around anyway. Definitely not the *valley of death,* she thought as she looked toward the quadrant that belonged to the god of war. The drawings of the city would have been fine, save that large charred circle. She didn't want to think what those pagan priests might have burned in their sacrificial fires. She felt uneasy about the geometric patterns of the third quadrant since she didn't understand them. They looked positively psychedelic. Which left her with the quadrant of fertility and love.

And Karim.

"Listen—" she began to say, but he was slipping into the water already.

She didn't dare move from the spot until he came

back ten minutes later. He pushed himself out of the water next to her then pulled a large bag after him.

The first thing he pulled out of the bag was his wallet. He took her passport out and handed it to her without a word.

She didn't understand why he was doing it, or why now, but wasn't about to question him. She took it without a word.

He held her gaze for a long moment. "Let's settle in for the night," he said.

"What do you think the missing item is?"

He shook his head. "Something of religious significance. Beyond that, I don't have a clue. Could be a chunk of meteorite. A ball of gold. An uniquely sized gem." He considered. "But probably not. I can't image a gem the size of a basketball."

"You think, whatever it was, Aziz took it?"

"We have to consider it likely."

"How do you think the bad guys knew what those idols look like?"

"Aziz probably made the drawing. He probably showed it to someone he shouldn't have."

She was only too aware even without the reminder that the idols peering at them in the semidarkness of the cave had been the death of Aziz. "And if we find the fifth component?"

"We'll take it with us, along with the others."

A gust of cold air ribboned through the cave as Karim spoke. Julia wrapped her arms around herself, feeling the chill of her wet clothes for the first time. And she shivered.

THE PLACE UNSETTLED him and mesmerized him at the same time. The same could be said about the woman sleeping next to him.

Karim watched her face in the light of the sole lamp they'd left burning. She had asked that they didn't turn off all the lights, and he was fine with that.

She whimpered in her sleep. What she'd been through since she'd met him—a car explosion, a car chase, being shot at—would probably give her nightmares for years to come. He sincerely regretted that. He wanted nothing more than to keep her safe, her and her baby.

She whimpered again, but while he debated whether to wake her from the dream or not, she opened her eyes on her own and after a moment they focused on him.

"Bad dreams?" He willed himself not to move closer. He'd nodded off, too, when they first turned in, and had seen his own share of dark images of a fight to the death, blood and destruction.

"I dreamed about the city."

"Baltimore?" It came as no surprise that she would be homesick.

But she shook her head. "The city drawn on the cave floor. I was running through the streets and people were chasing me."

"Who?"

"I couldn't tell. Dark figures. But I knew if they caught me, they would kill me." Her voice weakened on the last words.

He did move closer then, but stopped short of taking her into his arms. "I would never let that happen."

She still seemed shaken, and leaned toward him, looked up into his face. "Want to hear something strange? I had one of those robe dresses on."

"An *abaya?*"

"Kind of, but it was a lot fancier. Kind of sheer." She looked embarrassed as she said that. "And there were other people around, not a lot, but enough. I ran through some kind of a market. They were all looking at me."

He reached to her face to smooth the hair out of her eyes, intending only to skim her cheek if that. But she reached up and held his palm to her skin.

"Karim—"

Her eyes were dark and large in the dim light, her face the most beautiful thing he'd ever seen. He wanted her, had wanted her from the first second he laid eyes on her. For a moment yet, he fought the overpowering pull. Then he gave up the fight and kissed her.

Her mouth was warm and soft. A brief brushing of his lips over hers wasn't enough, just as skimming her cheek with his fingers hadn't been enough. And in that moment when she opened for him, he knew with clarity that nothing would ever be enough but having her fully, forever. She would have to be his wife and her child his own.

He put all that into the kiss, hoping she felt it, too, hoping she wouldn't put up too hard a fight while he tried to convince her.

She tasted like honey-cured figs, of which he'd had

copious amounts in his childhood. Now, like then, he couldn't get enough.

A deep fog of pleasure saturated his mind as he explored her mouth with his tongue, as he ran his fingers down her back, over her slender curves. His hand strayed to her abdomen, hesitantly, unsure how she would feel about that. But once again, she reached for him and held his palm over the life that was growing inside.

Something shifted behind his breastbone, and outside him, too, maybe. The air did seem to change in the cavern, hazier, thicker, as if some sort of an enchantment had descended over the pool and the flat plateau next to it where they had set up their sleeping bags.

He could almost swear he could smell the flowers drawn on the rock, and could hear the chirping of birds over the sounds of the waterfall that seemed quieter than earlier. An illusion, no doubt, because at the moment Julia was filling all his senses.

Their clothes seemed to fall away without much effort. There was not an awkward moment, not a doubt in him, just the sure knowledge that this was it, she was it, this was right.

When he moved over her, she parted her lean thighs with a smile, sighed in contentment as he tasted every inch of her skin. Time lost meaning. He spent a couple of years with her enlarged breasts that seemed extra sensitive.

Then out of all that easy pleasure a sense of urgency began to grow, and her body opened for him, accepted all of him, surrounded him with tight heat. They moved together to the sound of the water, swallowing each others' moans.

When her body contracted around him, he felt more than just his control shatter. They floated away on twin tides of bliss and satisfaction to a place from which he never wanted to return.

THEIR PASSIONATE lovemaking had been, in many ways, like a dream. Julia was still under its effects the next day, could barely believe it had been real as she was waited for a ray of light to penetrate the cavern's darkness.

The lights were off, so as to more easily spot the arriving sunlight. They talked. About the statues and old religions, about everything but what had happened in the night. And she was grateful for the darkness that made it impossible for Karim to see her face.

They had made love. And something between them had changed.

She wasn't going to ignore that. Ignoring never made any problems go away. But she needed some time to gather her thoughts. She was about to address the issue when Karim announced that the daylight was pretty much gone outside. And since there had been no light coming in, that meant that there were no cracks in the rock above them, no ancient, hidden signal to show them any new clues. They should be going back.

"Back, back? To Tihrin?" Relief flooded her. The cavern seemed different today. Colder. Darker. Some-how ominous. She'd gotten the distinct feeling that they had outstayed their welcome. When Karim slid into the pool, she didn't waste any time following him.

"It's more comfortable driving at night. The air is much cooler." He grabbed on to her hand and ducked under.

She followed him.

The way back was a lot easier than their way in, the current pushing them forward. She was breaking surface in less than a minute.

She got out and walked toward their equipment, intended to help him pack, but he stayed in the pool. "Are you bringing the idols over?"

"Just our things." He paused for a moment. "I think we should leave the idols here."

And strangely, some of the tension she'd been struggling with all day suddenly lifted. "Good idea." She felt that without a doubt. Now that she'd seen the idols, she didn't think they should bargain with them. They would have to come up with a new plan.

"Take a break. I'll be back in a minute." Karim slipped under the water.

She put her pants back on and borrowed a dry shirt from his bag then began picking up his tools, thinking about the strange night and strange day they had spent here. She could see their truck in the moonlight, parked in front of the cave's mouth exactly where they had left it.

She wasn't about to try and lift any of the larger crates, but she figured she could take small things over— a coil of rope, a couple of lamps. But when she put her hand on the truck's door handle, it wouldn't give.

Karim would be here in a minute.

But then a hand grabbed her shoulder from behind, and someone spoke harsh words near her ear she didn't understand, in a voice that was definitely not Karim's.

Chapter Ten

They dragged her aside, out of sight of the cave's opening, and Julia could see the beat-up Jeeps now, two of them, filled with enough dents and scratches to make her think they'd seen their share of desert battles.

"Julia?" Karim was calling for her from the cave.

The hand that stunk like tobacco tightened around her mouth, half covering her nose, too, making it difficult to breathe. She struggled only briefly before she felt something cold at her temple and gave up.

"Listen, I think—" Karim fell silent when he came into view. He went completely still, taking in the situation.

She had a pretty good idea what he saw. Her with a gun to her head and who knew how many men behind her. They hadn't allowed her to turn around.

The man who held her spoke in rapid Arabic. Karim didn't respond, but his face was getting darker with every passing second.

Since her captor still wouldn't let her mouth go, she couldn't say anything. She tried to communicate with her eyes. *Do something. Don't mind the gun. Don't let them take us.*

And for a moment, she saw Karim's muscles bunch, his powerful body shifting smoothly into a warrior's stance. More guns were cocked behind her. Her captor pressed the barrel of his gun to her skin so hard it hurt. People shouted.

Karim still hadn't said a word. But she could tell when he made his decision, a shadow shifting across his good eye. She did her best to groan out a *No!* as he lifted his arms to the side in a sign of surrender.

Two men came from behind her, carefully, rifles aimed at his heart. One strode behind him and shoved the rifle into the middle of his back, hard. Karim swayed, but two more slams were needed before the guy could send him to the ground, to his knees.

The other guy took Karim's car keys, and moved to his truck with two other men to search through it. They had probably already searched the cave. Ransacking the truck took them only a few minutes. When they came back, angry that they hadn't found what they were looking for, they wrestled Karim's hands behind his back and tied them.

Another strode into her view, an older man, his gray beard reaching to his paunchy abdomen. His robe was made of a finer material than the others', stark black, his bearing measured, despite the fact that his face was red with rage. He directed most of it at Karim and barked questions at him, one after the other, angered even further when Karim wouldn't respond.

At last, the man gave up and stepped toward Karim, fingered his wet hair and shouted something. Two guys ran up from behind her and disappeared into the cave.

At the same time, the men who held her thrust her forward, shoved her into the back of one of the cars. And she could finally see all the men, dressed in traditional robes and a full headdress, leaving nothing but their eyes showing.

Her hands, which had been simply twisted behind her, were getting tied now. Tight enough for the rope to scratch off some skin.

Shouts came from the cave, Arabic words she didn't understand. Then all the men ran in there, save two that stayed to guard them, their rifles aimed to shoot. Karim remained silent, and she followed his example. Twenty minutes passed and her arms began to ache from the unnatural angle the ropes twisted them into.

She couldn't take her eyes off the cave, waiting for the men to return, growing more and more uneasy when they didn't. Another twenty minutes passed. She became certain now that the men had found Karim's ropes and followed them to the pagan sanctuary on the other side of the underwater passage.

When the first man came out of the cavern with wet clothes, her heart sank. Then came the next and the next, the old man walking out last, cradling two idols in each arm like a mother cradling two sets of twins. But instead of love, hate burned in the man's eyes.

One of his men ran to him with a brown sack and he transferred the statues, his gaze scathing when he looked at Julia and Karim. Then he gave a brief order to his men and got into the first car. Karim was dragged over and shoved into the backseat.

"Whatever happens, I'm going to find you," he called back, and that earned him a smack with a rifle in the back of the head.

The car she was in followed the first. That was good. They were going somewhere together. But she had few illusions, knew they were in the hands of murderers.

She spent the first half hour of the ride in sheer panic, and it wore her out fast. She had to get a grip. Maybe she could distract herself by taking stock of the situation.

They'd been captured. But they hadn't been hurt. Yet.

Maybe the old man had a special plan. That didn't bode well for them. Or maybe the people who captured them wanted information on the fifth idol and thought Karim and she knew about it. She blanched at the thought of what they would be willing to do to get it.

She had nothing but the clothes on her back, no weapons. She could only guess the same about Karim. Her hair, too, was still damp from the pool, her braid unraveled. The water dripping from it had soaked her shirt. But the air was hot enough to dry it in another few minutes. And none too soon. She didn't miss the way the men were eyeing her top as it clung to her breasts.

The thin material didn't leave much to the imagination. Probably the reason they hadn't bothered to search her. It would have been great luck if she'd had anything, even a paring knife, but unfortunately she had nothing.

Which meant if she were to get her hands on a

weapon it had to come from someplace else. Like her captors. She spent the rest of the trip surreptitiously observing them.

Three men were in the truck with her. Three with Karim, plus the leader with the idols. Another man drove the delivery truck behind them. They were all armed as far as she could tell, with AK-47s and knives. She didn't think she was ready to handle a rifle just yet, but if the chance presented itself to get her hands on a knife, she would take it.

The drive seemed to last hours. The sun was getting high on the sky, the heat nearly unbearable even with the breeze moving through the doorless Jeep. She felt faint, her lips parched, sand gritting between her teeth by the time she spotted a town on the horizon.

Hope rose in her suddenly, strong and fierce. They were going into civilization. She'd been afraid that they'd be taken to the middle of the desert and summarily executed. But in a town, people would see them. Someone would recognize the sheik. Someone would help. She tried to swallow, to wet her mouth, getting ready to scream her head off as soon as they got within hearing distance of anyone.

Which happened later than she'd expected. The town had been farther than it seemed, the flat, homogeneous sand throwing off her sense of distance.

First she could make out the buildings in greater detail. They must have been approaching on the slum side. The houses were made of mud, in places nothing more than a fraying piece of carpet serving as a roof.

Poverty and a general lack of caring was stamped over everything she saw.

Then the people finally came into view. She leaned forward, caught sight of the unfriendly faces, the hard glares. Ninety percent seemed to be men, only a handful of cowed women here and there in frayed *abayas* who kept their heads down, not daring to meet anyone's eyes.

She had a bad feeling here, something that made her keep her mouth shut. Everyone they passed was armed to the point of overdoing it, ammunition belts hanging off them like garlands from Christmas trees.

The men in the Jeep with her tensed, too, and made sure their own weapons were displayed and their fingers on the trigger. They drove through narrow, winding streets where sewage ran openly, the stench unbearable. The few children she saw looked around either with vacant eyes or scared expressions, most of them with scars over their small bodies.

The heat and the smell were nearly too much to bear. If her hands weren't tied behind her back, her palms would have been over her mouth. As it was, she tried to breathe as shallow as she could.

They drove through a busy market and for a few minutes she lost sight of the other car. Then she breathed a sigh of relief when their Jeep came to a halt in front of a large, disheveled building, and she spotted the other vehicle already there. Empty.

"Out." One of the men shoved her roughly, and she tumbled to the sand.

"Please. You don't have to hurt me. I'll go." She was

afraid of what they would do to her, afraid not only for herself but for her baby.

The man shoved her again, this time through the doorway, then up the stairs, shoved hard even though she had sped her steps. She was pushed down a long hallway, then into a tiny, dingy room with bars over the glassless window. Then the door slammed shut behind her, and she could hear the lock sliding into place.

She waited for Karim. When a few minutes passed and they didn't bring him, she went to the window and looked out over the busy market. A few stands sold food. Most of them openly displayed weapons and what looked like used electronics. Stolen merchandise most likely.

Another ten minutes passed before she was willing to consider that Karim might not be coming. They had been separated. And she had no idea where he was, what they were doing to him. She didn't even know for sure that he was still alive.

THE REST OF THE DAY passed frustratingly slow for Julia, nothing happening but an old woman bringing her water. She had begged for help, to be told where Karim was, for food. The woman looked right through her with the vacant stare of a drug addict. She wasn't impressed by the plight of a foreigner. She looked like she would sell her own daughter for another hit—probably already had.

And she had nothing beyond the water jar, nothing Julia could have taken from her and used as a weapon. But at least she had some water, which she drank greedily, and one piece of new information. There was a guard in front of her door. She heard someone lock the woman in with her, then unlock the door again when the woman knocked to signal that she was ready to leave.

When the sun went down, two men came in, bringing an oil lamp with them. The one with the gray beard she already knew; he had put on a strange headpiece, looking like a leader of some religion. The other looked like all the other men she'd seen as they'd driven through town, a bandit through and through, but better dressed than most.

The old man watched her with naked hate in his small black eyes. The other one measured her up with some interest. She drew back, all the way to the wall, unsure which one to be more afraid of.

The old one spoke first, harshly, spit flying from his mouth, and made one decisive hand signal she couldn't interpret. The other one kept examining her thoughtfully.

The old man spoke again. The bandit responded this time. Rage contorted the old man's face, his full attention on his buddy now, as he protested. Seemed like they were in some sort of a disagreement about what to do with her.

Which suited her just fine. Any delay gave Karim more time to find her.

The old man was nearly shouting now, the other speaking more reasonably as if trying to convince and appease him. Finally, he pulled some money from his pocket, and the man of religion instantly mellowed. He was still shooting Julia hateful glances, but at least he was no longer yelling. He did say something, though.

The other guy looked her over one more time, then asked her one word. "Virgin?"

His accent was so thick she could barely understand. Then when she did, she was too shocked to answer.

"No lie. Will exam."

Over her dead body, she thought, knowing full well that could easily be arranged. She shook her head.

The man nodded. "No need exam." Then turned back to the other man and gave him another single bill, which made the old guy scowl and start arguing again.

She felt faint with hunger and with the realization that she was most likely witnessing her own sale. She had few illusions what for.

"I'm pregnant," she said without meaning to, the horror of the moment pushing the words out.

The man buying her merely shrugged. "Men no mind. If do, we fix."

All the blood ran out of her face, her hands cradling her abdomen, the barely there bump. *We fix.*

Oh, God.

She was, for the first time in her life, scared wordless. She could not utter a single syllable, not to beg, not to protest.

The men barely glanced at her when they left, the old man's gaze still holding hate, the other one's now glinting with satisfaction.

She sunk to the dirty floor when the door closed behind them.

She had come to Beharrain full of hope to find her child's father. But she had already lost Aziz without knowing it. And now she was about to lose everything else: her freedom, possibly her child, her life. Karim.

She wasn't sure when he'd begun to matter, but all of a sudden she knew that he did, more perhaps than any other man had mattered in her life.

Her arms wrapped around her abdomen, she stayed where she was and choked back her tears.

Soon the old woman came again, this time with a chunk of what looked like leg of lamb and some flatbread. And a dress. Julia ignored the latter but threw herself on the food as soon as the woman left. When she sucked the bone clean, she drank the last of her water. She'd been dehydrated all day, but now that she'd finished off a whole jar of water, she really, really had to go.

She knocked on the door. They had to let her out. No response. Knocked again. Banged. Nothing. The guard had probably been ordered to ignore her. Oh, great.

The room was dark now, the only faint light coming from the waning moon, what little the small window let in. The only things in there with her were the water jar, the lamb bone in the corner and the dress. Clearly, only one of those was suitable for her purposes. She did the deed, praying that she would be able to get out of here tonight, because she had a feeling that would still be the same jar they'd be using for her water tomorrow and she didn't think the drugged-out old crone was going to bother with rinsing it.

Getting out. Tonight. Fed and relieved, she could actually focus on escaping. She was exhausted, but there was nothing like the threat of being sold into prostitution to give a woman a little extra boost.

She moved to the bars and shook them. Since the bricks they'd been embedded in were mud, they wiggled a little, but not nearly enough. She needed a tool. She glanced at the water jar again. Nope. Not going there. Then her gaze settled on the lamb bone. She grabbed it up, ran her fingers over the knobby ends. Not exactly the best tool for digging through sun-hardened mud. She'd have better luck with her fingernails, which were growing strong and long from the prenatal vitamins. She needed something sharp.

Running her fingers over the metal bars gave her an idea. They were old and rough, almost like a metal file. She pressed the bone against one and dragged it along the abrasive surface a couple of times, felt again. Better. Ten minutes of work left her with one end of the bone as sharp as a knife. She scraped her new tool against the mud brick and some flakes of clay dropped to the ground. She smiled.

Then stepped away quickly and hid the bone behind her back when she heard her door being unlocked again.

KARIM LOOKED AT his torturers through the miniuscule slit in his swollen good eye. One more hit there and he'd be completely blind, a deep fear that had plagued him all through childhood.

"Who else knows about the idols?" the old man in the black robe asked again. "What do they mean?"

"Where is the woman?" he asked through bleeding, swollen lips.

They'd been through this script a couple of times. Next came the beating. The play did not improve with repetition.

Predictably, the man on his left slammed the butt of his rifle into Karim's face again. This time it hit his jaw, with nearly enough force to shatter the bone.

As it was, Karim felt his skin split. "I'll tell you everything I know in exchange for the woman." His words slurred through his swollen lips. He had no information to give. Mustafa—he'd learned the name the hard way—knew more than he did, had the fifth item in his possession already. It sat on a low table along with the four idols, a webbed globe of gold, enclosing an ancient human skull.

"I'll tell you everything," Karim said again. For the last fifteen minutes he had stayed alive by pretending that he had information that was crucial to the idols. "For Julia."

"There's no more woman!" the old man shouted, his eyes bulging with fury, the veins standing out at his temples.

Karim saw red, too, and not just from the blood that dripped down his forehead and into his eye. What the hell did he mean, there was no more woman? What in hell had they done to her?

He'd been biding his time, waiting for them to think he'd been beaten enough, waiting for them to let down their guard. One man leaving would have been enough. Or one man taking his damned rifle off him. Then he would move. That was the plan.

There's no more woman.

He rose from his knees with an enraged roar. To hell with the plan.

He caught the guy off guard, and managed to bowl him over. They crushed to the floor in a bone-jarring slam. He couldn't get to the gun at once, had to break the man's neck first. He didn't hesitate.

Nor did the others. Bullets flew at him from every direction. He caught sight of Mustafa from the corner of his eye as the man slipped out of the room; the rest of them were coming straight for him.

JULIA DROPPED her makeshift tool to the floor and stepped on it to cover it up. Whatever they did to her, she was not moving from that spot. But it was only the old woman who came in, with a lamp and a scowl on her face.

She pointed at the clothes she'd brought earlier and yelled at Julia. Apparently, she should have gotten changed.

She didn't want to think of the details of what might happen tonight. Couldn't afford to get bogged down in the sheer terror of that or it would paralyze her and she wouldn't have the strength to do what she needed to do to escape.

The old woman yelled at her.

The dress was in the other corner of the room. She couldn't move there without revealing the sharpened bone, which she was not willing to give up. She shrugged.

The woman hustled over, picked up the dress and tossed it at Julia.

The material was sheer, the golden silk ribbon around the hem and split neckline a little worn, but the fabric was clean. Still, it was such a ridiculous outfit that she held it away in distaste. Just the right thing to do to push the crone over the edge, it seemed, as the next second the woman was coming over, hooking a gnarled finger into the neckline of her tunic and ripping it all the way to the hem.

"Hey!"

The woman glared at her with all sorts of threats in her previously vacant eyes. She was in obvious need of a hit and was going to be as grouchy as she pleased until she got it.

Fine. Julia shook out the dress. If it would make the woman leave, she would put it on. She pulled the dress over her head. *Oh.* It was a lot more sheer than she had thought, leaving little to the imagination. Her bra showed clear through.

The woman clucked her tongue.

Julia wanted her to be gone so she could get back to her work. She could put on her other clothes later. She unhooked her bra and let it drop, crossing her arms in front of her to cover herself.

"Good enough?" she asked when the old crone still didn't look happy.

The woman glared at her slacks.

Oh, for heavens' sake. Julia lifted her left leg first, stepped out then let the material pool around her right foot, so when she stepped out of that side, the woman wouldn't see her secret lamb bone weapon.

And it still wasn't enough. What else did the hag want?

She made it clear when she stepped closer and reached under Julia's dress.

"Stop!" She held her hands out and put as much threat onto her face and into her voice as she could. She assumed the fighting stance she'd seen Karim do. She was *not* giving up her panties.

And the old crone must have understood that this here was the end of the line, because she grabbed the rest of Julia's clothes from the floor with a quick swoop, then disappeared from the room. Since she took her lamp with her, Julia was plunged into darkness again.

One deep breath was all she allowed herself, one second to gather her strength and determination, then another so her eyes could get used to the darkness again. When she could see a little better, she grabbed her tool and went back to work on the mud bricks.

An eternity passed before she got one end of one bar free. Maybe it would have been better to hold her sharp tool to the old woman's throat and hold her hostage, try to gain her release that way. Except she wasn't sure just what the old woman's value might be to her employer. Could be considerably less than the money the guy had just paid for Julia. Which meant, there could hardly be a trade.

She went to work on the next bar, scraping dried mud as quickly and quietly as possible. When she was done, she rattled the whole thing again. It didn't give much more than before. And her fingers were bleeding in three different places where she'd scraped them.

Once, she nearly cut into her own arm when the sharpened bone slipped. But she couldn't afford to slow down. Even at the frantic pace she worked, she wasn't going to scrape her way out, she was beginning to realize, not even if she had the whole night, which she seriously doubted.

They had fed and watered her, dressed her. She had a fair idea what was coming next.

Where was Karim? He had promised not to let anything happen to her as long as he lived. He hadn't come to see her all day. She tried not to dwell much on the thought that chances were good he was already dead.

He couldn't be. She needed to talk to him. They needed to discuss what had happened at the cave. She had to tell him how she felt about him. She had to get out. She had to call for help. She had to do something to save him.

Something scraped against the lock behind her. Were they coming for her already? Her heartbeat sped as the damn lock scraped again.

Here we go.

She faced the door and hid the sharp bone behind her back. The window was still impassable. She had two choices—fight now and be most likely killed, or go on and let them do whatever they wanted to do to her, in the hopes that later, a few days or weeks from now she might be able to escape and at least save her child. Unless they did something to her in the meanwhile that could cause her to lose her baby. *Oh, God. Please, not that. Anything but that.*

She was saved from having to make a choice when Karim burst into the room the next second.

One fleeting moment of hope was all she was allowed. Then she saw the army of bandits behind him.

Chapter Eleven

Karim slammed the door and turned the key he'd wrested from the guard, knowing it would give them only minutes of safety at best.

"Did they hurt you?" His heart thumped as he took her in, noticing the sheer dress. Black rage filled him. They had her dressed for— He didn't want to think that he might already be too late.

He focused on the fact that there were no visible signs of injury on her. Looked like they spared her the torture. And he knew why, and fury swirled out of control inside him.

She was staring at him in horror. "What happened to you?"

And he realized he probably looked like something that had come through the meat grinder. "Nothing serious." He handed her the bag of idols he'd managed to grab, then pushed her behind him and faced the door, holding the rifle, knowing he was dangerously low on ammunition.

Most of the men who'd tortured him were dead, but there were plenty of others in the building to take their place, and their leader in the black robe, Mustafa, was still alive and still wanted his head on a pike.

There were people outside, systematically trying to break down the door. He checked the rifle.

"How many bullets?" she asked from behind him.

"Six."

She put a slim hand on his shoulder. "I want you to save one for me," she said with gut-wrenching courage.

He turned around and saw that she was serious. More than anything, he wanted to draw her into his arms and promise her that everything was going to be fine. But he could make no promise beyond the one he had made before, that no harm would come to her as long as he was alive. Which might not be a long time, judging by how the door was creaking and splintering.

"When I run out, I'll get another weapon," he said.

"I have this." She extended a makeshift bone knife.

He looked at it then at her in surprise. "Good. Use it."

"I was trying for the window but didn't get far."

He moved to examine the bars for the first time. He hadn't paid much attention to them since he'd checked the ones in his own cell before his torture began and they were solid. But here he could see that she'd put serious effort into weakening them.

He handed her his weapon. "Hold this and stand by the door." Then he grabbed the bars and went to work on them.

Movement. There was definite give. He put all his

strength to wiggling the iron rods out of place, chunks of dried clay getting dislodged. He gave it a good shove. Then another. And the first bar came away in his hands. Then the next and the next.

When the hole was large enough to fit his head through, he looked out. There were shacks below, sharpened poles holding up frayed carpets with people settling in for the night underneath. They couldn't jump without risking being skewered by those poles. He looked up. The distance to the roof wasn't too bad.

"Come on." He pulled back into the room and took the rifle from Julia, hooked it over his shoulder and gave her a boost. "We're going up."

He didn't have to explain. She was already scrambling for the roof. He went after her just as the door broke into planks behind them.

"Go, go, go!" He pushed her to the flat clay tiles, grabbed her hand then ran with her. But they ran out of roof too fast, a six-foot gap between their building and the next. "Can you make the jump?"

"You bet." She pushed away without slowing down, which was the exact right thing to do.

He stumbled when they landed, too focused on keeping her with him. She didn't. This time, she was the one to tug him after her.

The first bullet coming from behind made them both duck. Then a whole buzz of them followed, and they jumped to a lower roof where they would be temporarily out of sight. They were at the edge of the market that was still not entirely deserted. A couple of people still strolled among the weapon stalls; others drank with their friends or played games of chance with goat-bone dice.

"What is this place?"

"Yanadar. Town of thieves and murderers." He growled the words as he considered the maze of stalls for a moment before slipping to the ground from the low roof and heading for it, Julia close behind. On the rooftops they had no cover. The maze of the market was what they needed.

A couple of the men loitering around piles of weapons looked up and reached for their guns. But the rifle in Karim's hand and the look in his nearly swollen-shut eye must have communicated his intent clearly, because not one chose to get involved in his business.

They ducked between stalls, ran through a couple, but their pursuers were close behind them, shooting at them at regular intervals. He knew he couldn't keep up the pace forever. They were not going to be able to outrun these men on foot, not when those bastards knew every path of the market by heart and he was half-lost already.

Then Julia tugged him to the right suddenly, and he knocked over an oil lamp as he adjusted course. He ran on without slowing to apologize.

"This way." Urgency rang clear in her voice.

It wasn't as if he had a better idea. She zigzagged through stalls, and he followed her without hesitation.

"What are we looking for?" he asked at the next turn.

She didn't respond for a while, and when she did, it

was with visible reluctance. "This is the market from my dream. There was a car this way."

And before he could even finish thinking how crazy that was, they came upon a beat-up pickup truck with two goats in the back. The driver's-side door was open, the key in the ignition. No owner in sight.

He didn't hesitate but pushed Julia into the car and over to the passenger side, hopped in behind her and took off before even closing the door.

"Which way out?" Maybe her dream had shown her that, too.

But she shook her head, hanging on to the dashboard for dear life as he flew over the potholes in the road. The trouble with the market was that it consisted of a hodge-podge of buildings, makeshift stalls mixed in with mud homes people clearly lived in, and the occasional large, multistory abode that must have belonged to the more successful thieves.

After a few minutes, he got the distinct feeling that he was driving around in circles. Then his choices became limited as he noticed light in the rearview mirror and realized that a part of the market was on fire, stalls going up in blaze. He drove in the opposite direction.

He reached the edge of the desert within minutes and stepped on the gas, following the makeshift road, having no idea where it led. Away from the fire and the men with guns was good enough for him.

For a while it looked like things were working, that they had successfully left their pursuers behind. Then dark spots dotted the sand behind them, and he realized that they were still being followed. Four vehicles, faster than his ancient pickup, were closing the distance.

When they got close enough, he could see that they were all jam-packed with armed men, at least two dozen of them.

He was outnumbered, outgunned and outsped.

He put all that from his mind and pressed the gas pedal to the floor. He knew what would happen when the men got within shooting range. They were out in the middle of the desert without cover. And those guys probably had fifty bullets to every one he had.

He took Julia's hand, sharing his attention between her and the barely visible road. "I'm sorry I dragged you into this. I should have let you go that first day."

She simply squeezed his fingers.

He would have felt better if she screamed at him.

"We don't have long, do we?" Her gold-brown eyes were filled not with fear, but with acceptance.

He couldn't say the word.

"I'm glad I met you," she said.

"I wanted you from the moment I first saw you. I told you that I kept you close to protect you, but deep down, I kept you for myself. I was selfish, and—"

"Last night at the cave was the best night of my life."

That shut him up for a few moments. He didn't deserve her.

"If things were different, I would have asked you to stay. Of your own free will. For me."

Her fine eyes misted a little. "If things were different, I would have."

Joy mixed with pain inside his chest until it felt like bursting, then anger at not being able to do anything about this.

He checked the rearview mirror and for a moment thought they had gained some ground, then realized that the reason he couldn't see the enemy's cars as good as before wasn't because they were farther back, but because the sky was darkening behind them.

"Roll up your window," he told Julia, and did the same.

"What is it?"

"Sandstorm." He wished he could give more gas, but the pickup was going at maximum speed already.

The storm was upon them in minutes, fast as a tornado and just as violent. He stopped the pickup and hung on to Julia while the wind rocked the car as if it were a toy. The sound of tons of sand hurling through the air was unbearably loud. They could see nothing beyond the windshield, had no idea how much sand had piled on top of them, whether they had been buried alive.

"The goats?" Julia attempted to go for the door.

He held her back. "They're animals. They have good instincts." Not that a severe sandstorm had never decimated a herd, but for the most, the animals were better equipped for inclement weather than humans.

He pulled her over to his side, into his arms. He didn't know how long they had, but every minute was a gift. The storm that stopped them would also stop their enemies, of that he was sure.

"I wish it would last forever." She snuggled against his chest.

The pain that still raked his body from Mustafa's torture disappeared as soon as they touched, but a new one was now building behind his breastbone. He was supposed to be able to protect the woman he loved. He pressed a kiss to her forehead, then to her lips when she lifted her head.

Her lips parted, and he tasted her, and felt the full grief of knowing he would be tasting her for the last time. Her breasts pressed against his chest. He locked his arms around her, not wanting to let her go, not ever.

They broke apart only for a moment, only to refill their lungs with air before coming together again. She pressed kisses along his right eyebrow. When he closed his eyes, she kissed his eyelid, then trailed her lips down his scar.

"I want to kiss all your scars," she said.

Not long ago, he would have been happy if a woman could just look at his scars without flinching. But those scars no longer mattered. The darkness of the past no longer bound him. And he knew without doubt that, somehow, Julia had done that to him.

"Forget the scars. I have no feeling in them anyway."

"Where should I kiss you then?" she teased.

"Anywhere you'd like," he said. "But I was hoping we weren't done yet with the lips." He could have kissed those lips of hers forever.

"Make love to me," she whispered into his ear a while later.

That, he could hear even over the storm that sounded like it was never going to stop. And when she reached down to pull her dress over her head, he helped her.

He slid over to the passenger side and she straddled him, her glorious breasts in line with his lips. He drank from them as if drinking life itself, and in a way, he was. She was his life, for as long as he had her.

Each caress, each kiss gained special meaning, was a bittersweet greeting and saying goodbye at the same time. His heart was filled to the brim with love he felt for her, with need that he had never felt for any other woman.

She set his body on fire, and he shoved off his clothes, wanting more than anything to be skin to skin. She lifted up, and he grabbed her hips, sheathed himself inside her tight heat, felt like he'd reached heaven and wanted to stay there forever.

They took it slow. The storm showed no signs of abating, and they both knew that this was all they were ever going to have. Their hearts melted together along with their bodies. He could feel all the darkness that had weighed his life down drift away. There was nothing and no one but Julia.

When the pressure built to the point of being beyond his control, his movements sped on their own, and Julia matched them, her head thrown back, her hair spilling down the sweet arch of her naked back, her breasts thrust upward. And they went over the edge together, then held on to each other for an eternity, until he could hear the storm quiet.

When the wind died altogether, he kissed her one last time, then put his clothes back on and gave his door a good shove. A few more were needed before it gave. He got out and looked for their pursuers. He couldn't see as far as before; there were still trillions of small particles of sand in the air, dimming the sun, making visibility worse. But he could see the men who'd followed them from the lawless bandit town of Yanadar.

They were down to three cars. One had been completely buried in the sand. And when he looked more carefully, he realized another one was at least half-buried. They would have trouble getting that out in a hurry.

He checked on the goats. They were shaking sand off their fur, looking nervous but unharmed. He walked up front and cleared off the windshield, pushing several buckets worth of sand off with his bare hands. Then he got back behind the wheel and gave thanks to Allah when the motor turned over on the first try.

The sandstorm completely covered what little road there had been, so he set out blindly. He couldn't even navigate by the stars as he couldn't see them. But they were definitely in better shape than they had been half an hour ago, he confirmed as he looked into his rearview mirror and saw that only two vehicles followed, overflowing with men, Mustafa in the passenger seat of the first car. Everyone from the buried cars had piled into and onto the remaining ones, adding considerable weight and slowing them down. The good news was that now they were matched for speed with Karim. The bad news was that they still outnumbered him a dozen to one.

It would all come down to who had more gas in the tank. He felt the first touch of optimism when he noted that his was three-quarters full. Then a pang of dismay when the first fat raindrop hit the windshield.

"Rain?" Julia sounded as surprised as he felt.

It wasn't the season for rain. The windstorm must have blown some clouds in from someplace far away. "It does rain, even in the desert. Just not a lot."

Another fat drop followed the first. And within minutes, they were in the middle of a downpour.

He headed toward the tall dunes to his right, not wanting to get caught in a low-lying area. An hour passed before he reached them, navigating by his headlights. The visibility in the dark night with the rain coming down like that was about the same as it had been in the sandstorm. When he reached the top, he shut off the truck. They were going to have to wait this out, too.

"Water," Julia said in a weird voice.

"Yes. Lots of it." He turned toward her and drank in her beauty, wondering how long the rain might last, ready to pull her into his arms again.

"The market was on fire," she said, apparently focused on something else entirely.

He shrugged. "I kicked over an oil lamp."

"The sandstorm. It's wind. Air."

He couldn't really focus on the sandstorm. His mind was filled to the brim with images of what they had done while waiting it out.

"Fire. Air. And now water." Gingerly, she held up the sack that hid the god statues. "Do you think—"

"Coincidence," he said, despite the unease that sent a small shiver down his spine.

"What would earth be? Quicksand?"

"Don't say that." He looked through the windshield, feeling decidedly uncomfortable now.

They waited out the rain in tense silence, each contemplating the impossible. They didn't have to wait too long. When the sky cleared and the stars came out, the rain having washed all the sand out of the air, he got out once again to survey the damage.

He could see nothing where the two cars had been, half a mile behind him in the low passage. Not the top of a car, not a radio antenna, not a single man. But some of the sand dunes on the other side were gone, the landscape rearranged. And suddenly he knew what had happened. Too much rain had come down all at once, the sand unable to absorb it that quickly. The wet sand had run like a mudslide, had buried the two vehicles and all the men inside them.

Not all. He swore as gnarled hands grabbed onto his ankles and yanked him off balance. Mustafa rolled from under the pickup. He must have crawled up to them in the storm unseen.

A curved dagger sliced the air in the direction of Karim's throat. He jerked out of the way. He understood now that Mustafa would never stop until he was dead. In Mustafa's mind, Karim was connected to evil just as Aziz had been, because of the idols.

"You have offended the One God. You must die." Mustafa got to his feet at the same time as Karim. He was between him and the truck, the rifle on the front seat.

Mustafa hadn't brought his. Could be the sand had jammed it when they'd gotten caught in the sandstorm.

Karim could see from the corner of his eye Julia lifting the weapon. He didn't dare to fully look at her, wanted Mustafa to forget all about her and focus on him. He feinted to the left, then lunged forward on the right side, caught the man in the middle and they went down.

Down, down, down. All the way to the bottom of the dune where muddy sand pulled at them. The side of the dune could still cave in and bury the both of them as it had buried Mustafa's last two cars.

He grabbed the man's right wrist, but the old man's zealous hate doubled his strength. Karim got on the bottom somehow as they rolled, the tip of the dagger less than an inch from his good eye.

Careful now.

He rolled Mustafa and they broke apart, then stood again.

Karim could feel every one of his broken ribs, every knife wound they had inflicted on him during his torture. He hadn't had food or water in nearly twenty-four hours. He was unarmed against a fanatic whose sole purpose in life was to kill him.

To the ball of pain that was his body, death might have been a relief.

Except that Julia was waiting for him on top of the dune. Doing more than waiting.

The next second, a bullet slammed into the sand between him and Mustafa. Karim stepped back. Would have been good to know just how good a shot she was.

It didn't matter at the end. Mustafa looked up at her, and the momentary distraction was enough to take the man down. This time, when they rolled, luck seemed to desert the old bastard as his dagger pierced through his clothes and skin, straight into his heart.

When Karim got back to the truck and took the rifle from a trembling Julia, he had her sit back in the cab while he checked around the tires and made sure the soil was stable. He had brushed off what Julia had said about fire, air, water and earth, but he couldn't shake his sense of unease. He'd seen quicksand up close and personal before, and he didn't care for seeing it again.

Looked like they'd run out of human enemies. He didn't want to have to face more of nature's peril on this trip. They'd had plenty enough adventures already.

He got back in and drove slowly, in the direction where the sand looked the most stable. He didn't dare breathe easily until he reached the edge of where rain had fallen and he was back on dry sand again, then on a rocky plateau he recognized. They had somehow gotten back to the area that hid his grandfather's cave.

In a few minutes, when the distinct shape of the rock above the cave came into view, Julia figured out where they were, too.

"Why did we come here? Shouldn't we ride straight to Tihrin?"

"We are putting the statues back," he said.

She offered no objections.

In five minutes they were at the cave, in another fifteen down at the pool in the first cavern.

"I'd like to go with you," she said.

And this time, he didn't argue.

They made it through the underwater passage without trouble—his rope was still stretched in place—and entered the second cavern. They were in complete darkness, had to go by feel.

"Stay right behind me," he said, and felt Julia's slim hand on his back. "The granite was straight ahead."

He walked that way until he hit the cave wall, groped around until he found the first niche. The rest was easier after that. He wasn't sure if he put the right statue in the right place and wasn't too concerned about it. He wanted to be out of there.

"Okay, now the skull." He reached up but couldn't feel the hole the last artifact belonged in. And the granite was a sheer vertical wall, no purchase for his feet anywhere to climb. "I'm going to have to lift you up."

She moved closer immediately. "What do you think the skull is about?" She'd already examined it up in the first cave.

"The skull of a tribal ancestor. Could be of some mythical hero." He handed her the golden piece, a shiver running down his back as the skull rattled inside, then lifted her up.

"I got it. It's in there," she said after a moment. "You can put me down."

He did so gently, passing up the opportunity to pause and hold her in his arms.

The first time they had come here, the cavern was a place of wonder. He had felt comfortable spending the night. Now the air pressed down on him, goose bumps rose on his skin and his only thought was to get out of there as fast as possible.

They stumbled toward the sound of the waterfall and that led them back to the pool. He slipped in first, caught Julia as she came after him, groped around for the rope.

"I got it," she said next to him and held his hand as they submerged.

They went back as quickly as they could. The journey home was always easier.

They didn't hang around in the first cavern, but went up the rope.

"I will talk to the queen and make sure she has the cave locked up and off-limits," he said.

Julia simply nodded thoughtfully. She didn't speak until they were in the car and he was pulling away from the cave.

"How do you know which way to go?"

He understood her question. The sandstorm and the rain had done a good job of obliterating the road. But he had the knowledge of his Bedu ancestors, the knowledge of the desert. "I can navigate by the stars."

They were about half a mile from the cave when the earth began to shake. And they watched in the light of the full moon, stunned, as dunes rose up and others sank, the landscape undulating before them like waves on the sea. He'd been through earthquakes, but never one in the desert.

He grabbed on to her when their car lifted, moving gently up, then down as the earth shifted beneath them. The whole thing lasted less than two minutes, leaving them both more shaken than the sandstorm and the rain put together.

"Are you all right?"

She didn't respond. Instead she was staring over his shoulder.

He turned, reaching for his gun at the same time. But it wasn't their enemies miraculously catching up with them again. It seemed they had been stopped for good, stopped forever, had stayed where they'd been, buried in the sand.

He blinked when he realized at last what Julia was looking at. The giant rock that had marked the cave was gone. Nothing but flat desert as far as the eye could see. He could hear Julia swallow behind him.

"I think that was the earth part," she said.

Epilogue

Five years later

Julia took another handful of postcards from the maid just as Karim strode through the door. As always, he took her breath away. And when he opened his arms to her, she walked into them.

He kissed her thoroughly, then bent to kiss her belly. "How is my little princess doing in there?"

"Impatient to come out. These are for you." Each summer, they received dozens of postcards from the Sibling Link Camp. Karim had donated Aziz's Star Island home to the charity. They, of course, immediately offered Julia her job back, but her hands were busy at the moment with other kid-related projects. She was, however, thinking about setting up a similar program here in Beharrain, had already talked about it to Queen Dara, who had pledged her support.

"How was your day?" She smoothed a dark lock of hair into place on his forehead.

"Good. And it's about to get better." He grinned and kissed her again. "I got an e-mail from the P.I. He traced your sisters to Texas. Looks like they were adopted together."

Her throat tightened. He had hired a top-rated agency to conduct the search for her lost sisters, no expenses spared. He had promised godmothers for their daughter. And when Karim promised something, he delivered.

"Thank you." She smiled at him, her heart filling with love and hope.

A smile hovered over his lips. "How grateful are you?"

She swatted his hand. "I'm too huge to be *that* grateful."

He gave her a tragic look that made her laugh. She kissed him. "I suppose I should show some gratitude." She nibbled his lips. That distracted them for a while.

"Almost forgot. Tariq is ready to show off his twin girls. We are invited tomorrow for dinner," he said when they reluctantly pulled apart.

"I can't wait to see them." The timing all worked out perfectly, her sister-in-law delivering just weeks before Julia was due. Their girls could grow up together. A cramp nudged her in the back. "I wish this kid was out already and *they* were coming to visit *us*," she said as her son, little Aziz, flew across the room and lunged himself at Karim.

"Are we going to the camel races, Dad? Are we leaving right now? I'm ready." He was a bundle of energy, deep dark eyes and dark hair, always ready for adventure. He was a happy child, always a smile on his face, secure in the knowledge that his parents, the rest of his large family and the tribe adored him.

"After lunch."

"I already had lunch. Mom let me have it early. I couldn't wait."

Karim crooked an eyebrow and put on his sheik face. "All your vegetables?"

"All." Aziz's face twisted with distaste.

"Your mom and I have to eat, too."

"You could have *maraq* at the races. You always say they make the best *maraq*."

"Maybe it will rain." Karim was teasing him now.

"Dad, it won't rain."

"What if we have a sandstorm? It's the season for it."

"We are not going to have a sandstorm," Aziz announced, full of confidence. And if he said it, they could believe it. He seemed to have a strange connection to inclement weather. "We could get some sweets after the *maraq*."

Julia smiled at her son, always a wheeler and dealer. She answered Karim's questioning look with a nod.

And her son caught that, of course, and lunged himself at her next. "Thank you, Mom!"

She kissed the top of his head before rubbing the dull ache in her back.

She had been organizing the new nursery all day—not that she couldn't ask the staff to do it. But arranging her daughter's things gave her so much pleasure. She'd rearranged the baby books on the shelves a dozen times, along with the stuffed animals at the foot of the crib; she'd looked at then refolded pink onesies and layette sets. The nursery was large and bright, one of the most beautiful rooms in the palace.

Her new home was a far cry from her cramped apartment in Baltimore. She didn't miss her old life—she was surrounded by love and family here. But she did miss her ache-and-pain-free body. Even a sheik's physician couldn't make that side of pregnancy disappear. She rubber her back again.

Karim immediately looked concerned, reaching for her arm. "Are you going to make it? We could stay home."

She smiled at the gentle way he touched her, at the love that shone in his gaze, her breath catching at the answering love in her heart. "Are you kidding me? She's her father's daughter. She would never interrupt a camel race."

And her smile widened as her firstborn whooped at hearing that.

* * * * *

Don't miss Dana Marton's
next fast-paced story of romantic suspense,
TALL, DARK AND LETHAL,
coming in December 2008,
only from Harlequin Intrigue!

Turn the page for a sneak preview of
AFTERSHOCK, *a new anthology*
featuring New York Times
bestselling author Sharon Sala.

Available October 2008.

n●cturne™

Dramatic and sensual tales
of paranormal romance.

Chapter

Chapter 1

October
New York City

Nicole Masters was sitting cross-legged on her sofa while a cold autumn rain peppered the windows of her fourth-floor apartment. She was poking at the ice cream in her bowl and trying not to be in a mood.

Six weeks ago, a simple trip to her neighborhood pharmacy had turned into a nightmare. She'd walked into the middle of a robbery. She never even saw the man who shot her in the head and left her for dead. She'd survived, but some of her senses had not. She was dealing with short-term memory loss and a tendency to stagger. Even though she'd been told the problems were most likely temporary, she waged a daily battle with depression.

Her parents had been killed in a car wreck when she was twenty-one. And except for a few friends—and most recently her boyfriend, Dominic Tucci, who lived in the apartment right above hers, she was alone. Her doctor kept reminding her that she should be grateful to be alive, and on one level she knew he was right. But he wasn't living in her shoes.

If she'd been anywhere else but at that pharmacy when the robbery happened, she wouldn't have died twice on the way to the hospital. Instead of being grateful that she'd survived, she couldn't stop thinking of what she'd lost.

But that wasn't the end of her troubles. On top of everything else, something strange was happening inside her head. She'd begun to hear odd things: sounds, not voices—at least, she didn't think it was voices. It was more like the distant noise of rapids—a rush of wind and water inside her head that, when it came, blocked out everything around her. It didn't happen often, but when it did, it was frightening, and it was driving her crazy.

The blank moments, which is what she called them, even had a rhythm. First there came that sound, then a cold sweat, then panic with no reason. Part of her feared it was the beginning of an emotional breakdown. And part of her feared it wasn't—that it was going to turn out to be a permanent souvenir of her resurrection.

Frustrated with herself and the situation as it stood, she upped the sound on the TV remote. But instead of *Wheel of Fortune,* an announcer broke in with a special bulletin.

"This just in. Police are on the scene of a kidnapping that occurred only hours ago at The Dakota. Molly Dane, the six-year-old daughter of one of Hollywood's blockbuster stars, Lyla Dane, was taken by force from the family apartment. At this time they have yet to receive a ransom demand. The housekeeper was seriously injured during the abduction, and is, at the present time, in surgery. Police are hoping to be able to talk to her once she regains consciousness. In the meantime, we are going now to a press conference with Lyla Dane."

Horrified, Nicole stilled as the cameras went live to where the actress was speaking before a bank of microphones. The shock and terror in Lyla Dane's voice were physically painful to watch. But even though Nicole kept upping the volume, the sound continued to fade.

Just when she was beginning to think something was wrong with her set, the broadcast suddenly switched from the Dane press conference to what appeared to be footage of the kidnapping, beginning with footage from inside the apartment.

When the front door suddenly flew back against the wall and four men rushed in, Nicole gasped. Horrified, she quickly realized that this must have been caught on a security camera inside the Dane apartment.

As Nicole continued to watch, a small Asian woman, who she guessed was the maid, rushed forward in an effort to keep them out. When one of the men hit her in the face with his gun, Nicole moaned. The violence was too reminiscent of what she'd lived through. Sick to her stomach, she fisted her hands against her belly, wishing it was over, but unable to tear her gaze away.

When the maid dropped to the carpet, the same man followed with a vicious kick to the little woman's midsection that lifted her off the floor.

"Oh, my God," Nicole said. When blood began to pool beneath the maid's head, she started to cry.

As the tape played on, the four men split up in different directions. The camera caught one running down a long marble hallway, then disappearing into a room. Moments later he reappeared, carrying a little girl, who Nicole assumed was Molly Dane. The child was wearing a pair of red pants and a white turtleneck sweater, and her hair was partially blocking her abductor's face as he carried her down the hall. She was kicking and screaming in his arms, and when he slapped her, it elicited an agonized scream that brought the other three running. Nicole watched in horror as one of them ran up and put his hand over Molly's face. Seconds later, she went limp.

One moment they were in the foyer, then they were gone.

Nicole jumped to her feet, then staggered drunkenly.

The bowl of ice cream she'd absentmindedly placed in her lap shattered at her feet, splattering glass and melting ice cream everywhere.

The picture on the screen abruptly switched from the kidnapping to what Nicole assumed was a rerun of Lyla Dane's plea for her daughter's safe return, but she was numb.

Before she could think what to do next, the doorbell rang. Startled by the unexpected sound, she shakily swiped at the tears and took a step forward. She didn't feel the glass shards piercing her feet until she took the second step. At that point, sharp pains shot through her foot. She gasped, then looked down in confusion. Her legs looked as if she'd been running through mud, and she was standing in broken glass and ice cream, while a thin ribbon of blood seeped out from beneath her toes.

"Oh, no," Nicole mumbled, then stifled a second moan of pain.

The doorbell rang again. She shivered, then clutched her head in confusion.

"Just a minute!" she yelled, then tried to sidestep the rest of the debris as she hobbled to the door.

When she looked through the peephole in the door, she didn't know whether to be relieved or regretful.

It was Dominic, and as usual, she was a mess.

Nicole smiled a little self-consciously as she opened the door to let him in. "I just don't know what's happening to me. I think I'm losing my mind."

"Hey, don't talk about my woman like that."

Nicole rode the surge of delight his words brought.
"So I'm still your woman?"

Dominic lowered his head.

Their lips met.

The kiss proceeded.

Slowly.

Thoroughly.

* * * * *

Be sure to look for the
AFTERSHOCK *anthology next month, as
well as other exciting paranormal stories
from Silhouette Nocturne.
Available in October wherever books are sold.*

Silhouette®

nocturne™

NEW YORK TIMES BESTSELLING AUTHOR

SHARON SALA

JANIS REAMES HUDSON
DEBRA COWAN

AFTERSHOCK

Three women are brought to the brink of death…
only to discover the aftershock of their trauma has
left them with unexpected and unwelcome gifts of
paranormal powers. Now each woman must learn to
accept her newfound abilities while fighting for life,
love and second chances….

Available October wherever books are sold.

www.eHarlequin.com
www.paranormalromanceblog.wordpress.com

SN61796

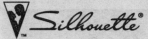

Romantic
SUSPENSE

**Sparked by Danger,
Fueled by Passion.**

USA TODAY bestselling author

Merline Lovelace

Undercover Wife

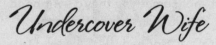

Secret agent Mike Callahan, code name Hawkeye,
objects when he's paired with sophisticated
Gillian Ridgeway on a dangerous spy mission
to Hong Kong. Gillian has secretly been in love
with him for years, but Hawk is an overprotective
man with a wounded past that threatens to
resurface. Now the two must put their lives—
and hearts—at risk for each other.

Available October wherever books are sold.

Visit Silhouette Books at www.eHarlequin.com   SRS27601

Three women. Three fantasies.

Years ago, Gemma, Zoe and Violet took the same college sex-ed class, one they laughingly referred to as Sex for Beginners. It was an easy credit—not something they'd ever need in real life. Or so they thought...

Their professor had them each write a letter, outlining their most private, most outrageous sexual fantasies. They never dreamed their letters would be returned to them when they least expected it. Or that their own words would change their lives forever...

Don't miss

Stephanie Bond's

newest miniseries:

Sex for Beginners

Available in October, November and December 2008 only from Harlequin Blaze.

www.eHarlequin.com   HB79432

REQUEST YOUR FREE BOOKS!

2 FREE NOVELS PLUS 2 FREE GIFTS!

◆ HARLEQUIN®
INTRIGUE®

Breathtaking Romantic Suspense

YES! Please send me 2 FREE Harlequin Intrigue® novels and my 2 FREE gifts (gifts are worth about $10). After receiving them, if I don't wish to receive any more books, I can return the shipping statement marked "cancel." If I don't cancel, I will receive 6 brand-new novels every month and be billed just $4.24 per book in the U.S. or $4.99 per book in Canada, plus 25¢ shipping and handling per book and applicable taxes, if any*. That's a savings of close to 15% off the cover price! I understand that accepting the 2 free books and gifts places me under no obligation to buy anything. I can always return a shipment and cancel at any time. Even if I never buy another book from Harlequin, the two free books and gifts are mine to keep forever.

182 HDN EEZ7   382 HDN EEZK

Name	(PLEASE PRINT)	
Address		Apt. #
City	State/Prov.	Zip/Postal Code

Signature (if under 18, a parent or guardian must sign)

Mail to the Harlequin Reader Service:
IN U.S.A.: P.O. Box 1867, Buffalo, NY 14240-1867
IN CANADA: P.O. Box 609, Fort Erie, Ontario L2A 5X3

Not valid to current subscribers of Harlequin Intrigue books.

Want to try two free books from another line?
Call 1-800-873-8635 or visit www.morefreebooks.com.

* Terms and prices subject to change without notice. N.Y. residents add applicable sales tax. Canadian residents will be charged applicable provincial taxes and GST. Offer not valid in Quebec. This offer is limited to one order per household. All orders subject to approval. Credit or debit balances in a customer's account(s) may be offset by any other outstanding balance owed by or to the customer. Please allow 4 to 6 weeks for delivery. Offer available while quantities last.

Your Privacy: Harlequin is committed to protecting your privacy. Our Privacy Policy is available online at www.eHarlequin.com or upon request from the Reader Service. From time to time we make our lists of customers available to reputable third parties who may have a product or service of interest to you. If you would prefer we not share your name and address, please check here. ☐

HI08R

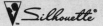

SPECIAL EDITION™

BRAVO FAMILY TIES

Tanner Bravo and Crystal Cerise had it bad
for each other, though they couldn't be more
different. Tanner was the type to settle down;
free-spirited Crystal wouldn't hear of it.
Now that Crystal was pregnant, would
Tanner have his way after all?

Look for

HAVING TANNER BRAVO'S BABY

by *USA TODAY* bestselling author
CHRISTINE RIMMER

Available in October wherever books are sold.

Visit Silhouette Books at www.eHarlequin.com   SSE24927

HARLEQUIN®

INTRIGUE°

COMING NEXT MONTH

#1089 CHRISTMAS SPIRIT by Rebecca York
A Holiday Mystery at Jenkins Cove
Some say old ghosts haunt Jenkins Cove, but not writer Michael Bryant.
Can Chelsea Caldwell change his mind—or will ghosts of Christmas
past drag the young couple to their doom?

#1090 PRIVATE S.W.A.T. TAKEOVER by Julie Miller
The Precinct: Brotherhood of the Badge
Veterinarian Liza Parrish was nobody special—until she witnessed the
murder of KCPD's deputy commissioner. Now she had the city's finest
at her disposal, but only needed their bravest, Holden Kincaid, to keep
her from harm.

#1091 SECURITY BLANKET by Delores Fossen
Texas Paternity
Quinn "Lucky" Bacelli thought saving Marin Sheppard would be the
end of their dalliance. But then she asked him for protection from her
domineering parents. And to pretend to be the father of her infant
son....

#1092 MOTIVE: SECRET BABY by Debra Webb
The Curse of Raven's Cliff
Someone had taken Camille Wells's baby. It was now up to recluse
Nicholas Sterling III to help the woman he once loved and right his
past wrongs if he was to save the town from the brink of disaster.

#1093 MANHUNT IN THE WILD WEST by Jessica Andersen
Bear Claw Creek Crime Lab
Federal agent Jonah Fairfax was in over his head, maintaining his cover in a
Supermax prison. But when some escapees abducted Chelsea Swan, Jonah
was ready to show his true colors in order to save the medical examiner's
life.

#1094 BEAUTIFUL STRANGER by Kerry Connor
Doctor Josh Bennett couldn't deny a woman in distress. Now he had to
help Claire Preston uncover the secrets of her past before a hired killer
put them both down for good.

www.eHarlequin.com

HICNM0908